1985

STORI3S FROM SØS

1985

STORI3S FROM SØS

E.C. MYERS

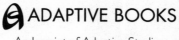
ADAPTIVE BOOKS

An Imprint of Adaptive Studios

Culver City, CA

Visit us on the web at www.adaptivestudios.com

Library of Congress Cataloging in Publication Number:
2017934245

B&N ISBN 978-1-945293-30-6

Ebook ISBN 978-1-945293-42-9

Printed in USA.

Designed by Torborg Davern.

Adaptive Books
3578 Hayden Avenue, Suite 6
Culver City, CA 90232
10 9 8 7 6 5 4 3 2 1

ALSO BY

E.C. MYERS

The Silence of Six

Against All Silence

For the next generation of dreamers, activists, misfits, rebels, and troublemakers.

We made this world, but you can change it.

CONTENTS

INTRODUCTION

WHEN I BEGAN WRITING *The Silence of Six* in 2014, my greatest challenge was staying ahead of the headlines.

In researching and plotting a book about hackers, corruption, government conspiracies, data leaks, and rigged presidential elections, I thought I was straddling the line between realism and near-future science fiction—but nearly every shocking development I came up with seemed to be happening or coming true, from revelations about Facebook's experiments in manipulating users to Edward Snowden's exposure of mass surveillance on a global scale.

It was important for me to represent hacking and its unique culture authentically and respectfully—as opposed to Hollywood's typical portrayal of hacking as magic—and tell a story that was believable, if not necessarily plausible. As of this writing, in January 2017, facts (and even "alternative facts") seem far stranger and unbelievable than fiction. The two novels in the SØS series, *The Silence of Six* and *Against All Silence*, now seem like contemporary thrillers rather than cautionary tales, and they are very much products of the interesting times we live in.

Knowing what we know now, I don't think I could write those books today, or at least they would be very different.

Normally I would argue that authors should let the writing speak for itself, but it seems fitting that I add a little context to the three stories in this collection. Each of them gives a voice to characters who were central to the SØS novels but usually took a backseat to the protagonist, Max Stein: Evan Baxter (aka "SØS"); Penny Polonsky (aka "DoubleThink"); and Max's parents, Bradley and Lianna Stein (aka "1985").

That's right. Max's parents!

The Max we know would not exist if those people had not influenced his life, helping him to figure out who he is and who he wants to be.

As returning readers will know, the first book, *The Silence of Six*, follows Max Stein and teenage hacktivists Penny and Risse Polonsky as they investigate suspicious deaths connected to a popular social media site—and the upcoming presidential election. The sequel, *Against All Silence*, takes place a year later. Max and Penny struggle with the sobering realization that they haven't changed things as much as they had hoped. They also have different ideas about how to deal with the latest threat to the personal freedoms of everyone in the world: a multimedia empire that is systematically taking over the internet and controlling information.

Even if this is your first foray into the SØS series, these events might sound familiar!

In *The Silence of Six*, Max's best friend, Evan Baxter, sets everything in motion by giving Max and Penny sensitive information and then killing himself live on TV. Although he only appears in chapter one, he was a huge part of the story through all its twists and turns—and how Max and Penny relate to these events and each other. I wanted to give readers a chance to get further into Evan's head, so the first story in this collection, "SØS," shares his final actions in the twenty-four hours before he takes his life, as both a prequel and a companion to the first novel.

Penny is central to both *The Silence of Six* and *Against All Silence*, and she was one of my favorite characters to write, ever. When I finished the second novel she demanded to tell her story too—which led to the middle story in this collection, "DoubleThink." This is a standalone adventure that bridges *The Silence of Six* and *Against All Silence*, in which Penny faces a mysterious new challenge that could change her life—and potentially the internet—forever. Right now, it feels particularly important to give her the stage in "DoubleThink" because media needs to highlight more women who are interested in and excellent at tech. Plus she not only is a kick-ass female protagonist™, but she really has her act together—maybe even more than Max.

Even as the SØS series focuses on current technology and looks ahead to its implications for the future, it's also deeply rooted in the past. Exploring the origins of hacking and the internet are prominent features in these stories, along with a certain nostalgia for pop culture of the 1970s and '80s, and the third story in this book, "1985" (with apologies to George Orwell), brings everything full circle.

This brand-new novella was written just for the *1985* collection. It introduces us to Max's parents, Bradley and Lianna, as teenagers in the '80s. They meet at a political protest in New York City, hatch a risky plan to expose unethical practices at Bradley's university, and begin to fall in love. In the early days of the internet, they become proto-hacktivists of a sort, and their escapades give new meaning to "underground movement"—taking them into the elaborate network of tunnels beneath Columbia University.

I have loved working on this series. The process taught me enough about hacking, computers, and surveillance to instill a healthy sense of paranoia every time I check my email, and it was fun to share some of the geeky things I enjoy with readers. Writing these stories has made me more engaged and interested in politics and the world around me, and interested in being more active in protecting the rights and improving the lives of everyone.

If reading the SØS books makes you a little more curious about technology or programming, informs you of real-life threats to safety and privacy, or motivates you to ask questions and change the world yourself, then I'm incredibly humbled and grateful for the opportunity to make some small impact with my words. But most of all, I hope you enjoy the characters and their journey through the World Wide Web, to the darkest corners of the internet and beyond. This collection was written for and is dedicated to you. Thanks for coming along for the ride.

—*E.C. Myers, January 23, 2017*

SØS

TUESDAY

2:00 P.M.

EVAN BAXTER WALKED AROUND THE block for a third time. His head was down and his hood was up, but he studied the cars and the people on the street closely. By all appearances, it was just another ordinary, boring Tuesday afternoon in downtown Granville. The only suspicious activity came from Evan himself, who was walking in circles and hauling a large black backpack that he swore got heavier each time he completed a circuit. He hiked the bag up on his shoulders and continued counting his steps. Ninety-nine or one hundred? He froze and struggled with the decision to go back and start over.

It was a cool October day, but Evan's face was pouring sweat and his balled hands crammed in the pockets of his cargo pants were clammy and trembling. He concentrated on holding them steady, squeezing his hands tighter. Control. That was better.

Maybe I'm coming down with something, Evan thought. *A virus.*

He laughed out loud, but the young mother pushing a stroller didn't even glance at him as she passed. (Evan confirmed the stroller held a sleeping boy, not a lifelike doll. She was *probably* a real mom running errands.)

Everyone talked or laughed to themselves those days; it was almost impossible to tell whether the man laughing his head off was mentally ill or talking to someone on his phone through the magic of Bluetooth. (Why couldn't it be both?)

Evan abruptly stopped laughing. He forced a smile, but then he decided that it wasn't necessary and relaxed his expression again. He worked hard to keep it all straight, wearing the face that people expected from him. Emoji were more straightforward and efficient.

Time was running out. He decided he had taken one hundred steps, but doubt still wormed its way to the back of his mind. He started walking again. *One-oh-one, one-oh-two, one-oh-three. . . .*

Evan should have stood out with his red sweatshirt and stuffed bag, but he was used to being overlooked or outright ignored. That was better than the alternative: being mocked for acting different. Evan was content to go about his life relatively unnoticed, which made his mission that much more difficult. After today, everyone would know him. He liked anonymity:

He lived on the internet, which eliminated his real-life awkwardness and shyness. He even enjoyed a measure of popularity online, or at least notoriety.

Satisfied that he wasn't being watched or followed (he glanced over his shoulder one more time), Evan slipped between the abandoned bookstore and the costume shop and hurried down the narrow alley to the parking area behind them.

Granville swarmed with Secret Service agents for tonight's presidential debate at the high school, so he acted cautiously. This was too important to mess up, and he couldn't risk being stopped. (Or maybe he wanted someone to stop him. He wasn't afraid for himself, but of what might happen to everyone else if he failed.)

Evan slipped off his backpack and set it at his feet. He lifted a loose, graffiti-covered plywood board and nudged the bag inside with one foot. He took one last look around his familiar stomping grounds before ducking through the low opening, then slipped into darkness.

MONDAY

9:12 P.M.

EVAN HIT THE ZONE. His fingers flew across the keyboard, spilling forth code in an exhilarating stream of letters, and numbers, and symbols.

His best friend, Max Stein, often talked about being in the zone on the soccer field, when everything but the ball and the net and the other players dropped away and his body performed a complicated series of physical feats he could never explain in words. Evan was no athlete (his arms and legs had minds of their own when he was forced to play sports in gym), but he was the MVP when it came to anything related to computers.

When he programmed, his thoughts became commands that computers translated into reality. Hacking wasn't magical the way Hollywood made people think it was, but, in the right hands, with the right code, the distinction was meaningless. If you dreamed of being a superhero (or a supervillain), it was the closest you could get in the real world, outside of comic books and blockbuster movies. Evan's superpower was in his brain.

But the doctors (even his parents, too) thought his mind was damaged in some way, that he had been born *wrong*. His mother, Allie, blamed herself, though she'd had about as much control over her genetics as Evan did. His father, Tony, never blamed himself for anything; he had yet to encounter a problem he couldn't fix with money, and he thought this one could be solved that way too.

His parents didn't see that Evan was who he was *because* of his genes: You could diagnose him and give his condition a name, but whether you called it Asperger's or autism or whatever, it was just Evan. He had his own name for it: STOP, his online handle. His true identity. That's who he really was.

Experts tried to treat Evan's "disability" with medication to calm his anxiety, to give him better focus. (He had no trouble focusing—just not on what his parents and teachers thought he should be focusing on.) But to Evan, those green pills were like tiny doses of Kryptonite. They changed him, but they didn't fix him. He wasn't better with them, he was . . . *less*.

Evan hadn't taken his drugs in the last few months, because they made him slow and dull and flat when he needed to focus and plan and put all the pieces together. He knew his anxiety was real; just because you're paranoid doesn't mean someone isn't after you. People had been murdered to be kept quiet because Evan had put them in jeopardy. And Evan would be next if he didn't stop their killers. Stop them. Stop. STOP.

He was almost done with the code. As he wrote (and rewrote) the final lines (which altered the worm's original purpose, the way the pills reprogrammed him), Evan hit the keys harder and faster, like a pianist reaching the crescendo of his magnum opus. If his parents had been home, they would have told him to keep it down. He sometimes woke them up late at night with his typing, even though he was all the way at the top of the house. It was part of the reason he was in the attic instead of his old bedroom one floor down, which was now his mother's little-used sewing room. But when it was in use, sometimes the sewing machine and his keyboard made a beautiful racket together.

Now, because of the loud, rhythmic sound of his mechanical keyboard and the loud, rhythmic sound of the music playing on his headphones, he almost missed the ding of his messaging program.

Evan switched to his chat window and felt a mixture of disappointment and excitement when he saw who was interrupting his flow. He'd been hoping for a communication from his only ally in this, Infiltraitor. But instead it was DoubleThink.

Excelsior!, STOP typed.

Whatever that means. Try saying hi, STOP.

HI, STOP typed. What do you want?

Evan stared at the terminal just under the chat window. He was so close to finishing, he itched to ignore DoubleThink and get back to it. But he also wanted to talk. He *needed* to talk, to someone.

He picked up his phone to check for text messages he might have missed while working. Still no response from Infiltraitor. Or Max.

sigh Just wanted you to know that the eagle has landed, DoubleThink typed. I'm listening to it now.

Good, STOP typed.

Like! Except for Telephone. Didn't figure you for a Gaga fan.

Just the mention of the title popped the song's lyrics into his head. "We're sorry, we're sorry. The number you have reached is not in service at this time."

Error 503. Service Unavailable.

Evan pulled off his headphones, releasing the sound of deadmau5's "Right This Second" from his head and into the real world. It was a good song and he wanted to put it on another CD for DoubleThink, if he ever had the chance. He had three other songs he wanted to include, and he wondered what new music would be out next week, next month, next year, that he might miss.

The pulsing music broke the funereal silence of the otherwise empty house, and he rushed to click it off. All he was left with was the humming electronics that made his attic bedroom seem alive with energy. He thought of it as the brains of the house, the control center, tapped into the digital world and connected to systems, peoples, and cities all over the globe.

I'm actually having some trouble figuring out these other files you sent, DoubleThink typed.

You'll get it, STOP typed. I believe in you. I trust you.

Duh. Hey, stop rocking. ;)

Evan paused and realized that he had been rocking back and forth in his chair.

DoubleThink couldn't see him—his computer security was too good for his webcam to be hacked, and DoubleThink wouldn't make the attempt on a friend, or at least not on Evan. The comment just reinforced what he already knew: to certain people, he and his actions were predictable. He took comfort in that and relied on it, because it was the only way his backup plan would work.

Evan was already thinking ahead, splitting reality into two scenarios. In one, a perfect world, Infiltraitor was still alive, biding his time. He wasn't dead, just lying low like he'd hinted at. He had been getting Evan's increasingly urgent, increasingly reckless messages, and was going to be in position tomorrow night to receive the computer worm Evan was programming and then deliver it where it could do the most damage. But he hadn't heard from Infiltraitor since he'd sent Evan the key, which had led Evan to believe he was on his own.

In another, more likely scenario, Evan would have to secure the precious computer worm like a hidden treasure, providing clues and a map that would hopefully lead the right people to it and keep it away from the enemy.

503-ERROR will know what to do, **STOP typed.**

Why don't you just tell me what's going on instead of pulling this cryptic shit? You know I don't have patience for it, **Double-Think typed.** Are you okay?

A patient waiter is no loser, STOP typed.

Evan didn't want to answer DoubleThink's question, and his thoughts had a tendency to wander. So he responded with the first thing that came to mind.

Did you know that when telephones first came into wide use, boys were originally hired as switchboard operators? They had been superb telegraph operators, but they got bored easily and they started cursing at customers and pulling pranks. So companies started hiring women instead. They had better manners.

Cool, DoubleThink typed. Did *you* know that the first woman telephone operator was named Emma Mills Nutt? Women were actually hired because they could be paid less and controlled more.

How do you know that? STOP typed.

How do you not? DoubleThink responded. Emma was hired by Alexander Graham Bell, and her sister Stella became the second telephone operator. They were the first two sister telephone operators ever.

Cool, STOP typed. Embarrassed that he hadn't heard of the Nutt sisters before (DoubleThink wouldn't make up a fact just to impress him), he countered with another bit of trivia. Did you know that the Morse code for SOS was introduced by Germany on April 1, 1905?

April Fools' Day? DoubleThink typed. Your favorite holiday.

STOP continued, But it wasn't used until four years later.

On the Titanic? DoubleThink typed.

Titanic was 1912, **STOP responded.** Its senior wireless operator, Jack Phillips, actually used the old distress signal, CQD. But he switched to SOS when he realized he might never get another chance to use it.

Evan tapped out the SOS code on his desk with his knuckles. *Dit dit dit. Dah dah dah. Dit dit dit.* He liked the sound of it.

He kept it up until he heard the front door open and close downstairs. He heard steps in the foyer, creaks on the floorboards.

Someone was in the house.

He looked around wildly at the machines around him, each of them filled with damning evidence of his extracurricular activities and worse: an irreplaceable and dangerous computer program that had to be protected at all costs.

brb, STOP typed. *I hope*, he thought.

Evan turned off his desk lamp and rushed to the window, peering down onto the street. Had that dark sedan been there before? Did it belong to the neighbors?

He returned to his desk and opened a new terminal. With shaking hands, he typed in the command that would start a countdown to wipe his networked computers, erasing all the evidence and his work along with it:

```
/var/root/.tmp0/self_destruct.sh --sequence destruct0
--code a1b1c1 --destruct0
```

He hesitated for only a moment before he hit ENTER. A three-minute countdown started, red digits flashing on all his screens. If he didn't cancel the program before his time was up, his computers would be lobotomized.

Game over.

Evan crept down the stairs, past the second floor, toward the living room. He moved silently, shifting his weight to the railing and bypassing the creaky steps that would betray him. He picked up a warped umbrella that leaned by the hall closet and brandished it, even though he knew it would be equally useless against both bullets and a Federal arrest warrant.

He glanced at the front door. He could run, but he wouldn't get halfway across the yard before being captured. He turned toward the living room. He wanted to see the people who had been hunting him and his colleagues.

He stepped inside.

"Evan!" Allie Baxter beamed at Evan. As she took in the umbrella cocked over his shoulder like a baseball bat, she frowned. "Honey?"

"Damn, Allie. What are you doing home?" Evan blurted out.

Allie and Tony were supposed to be on a business trip until the day after tomorrow. They were supposed to be *safe*, and he was supposed to have plenty of time to do what he had to.

Tony Baxter emerged from behind the bar with a glass of wine. "Good to see you too, son. What, were you planning to throw a party while we were out?" He chuckled and glanced at his wife. "Maybe you have a girl upstairs?"

"*Tone*," Allie warned.

"Shit," Evan said. "Damn!" He threw the umbrella across the room. It landed on the sofa with a soft thump. He didn't even have the satisfaction of breaking something.

He smoothed the rage from his face and tried to look apologetic. "You surprised me."

"You don't say." Allie unwrapped her scarf.

"I wasn't expecting you back this late," Evan said.

"Plans change. A board meeting got moved up so we had to rush back." Tony tossed back the rest of his drink and looked back toward the bar.

Now Evan had to change *his* plans. He had to move everything.

He spun around and bolted back upstairs, only tripping once and banging his knee on the top step. He reached his room and typed in the cancel command, with thirty-three seconds to spare.

DoubleThink: STOP? Are you there?

TUESDAY

2:24 P.M.

ALTHOUGH THE STORE HAD BEEN gutted over a year ago, the smell of musty pages and old bookbinding glue still lingered, stronger even than the aroma of dried beer and urine from squatters who had found their way inside before him.

Evan patrolled the store like a ghost, moving among bare shelves, breathing in stale air and blaming the dust for the tears stinging his eyes. He had not cried when his friends had been killed (he hadn't even met them in real life), and he wasn't crying now. He couldn't have any distractions.

There was no one else inside, and there was only one entrance—the way he had come in. (There was only one exit, too. No, there was another way out. He was not going to cry.)

Evan dragged a rickety table over to a clear corner, kicking away a shriveled condom that looked like a snake's discarded skin. He methodically pulled things from his backpack and set them up. His main laptop, Rorschach. Two small LCD screens. A small lamp. A portable generator. A webcam. His favorite keyboard. His cell phone. His mask.

He tucked his bag under his chair so it was within easy reach.

He'd meant to do this at home, but maybe it was better here. His parents wouldn't have to clean up after him. He had already erased all his other machines, certain he wouldn't be going back there.

He checked the clock on his phone. (No messages.) There was still a little bit of time, but he had a lot to do. Evan dragged over a chair and sat down to get to work. He plugged in his 4G USB modem and got online, checking his backdoor access to Granville High School's computer and video systems. He pulled up the security camera footage for the auditorium and displayed that on one of his screens. A few men and women in suits were sweeping the room, Secret Service agents performing their final safety checks. Seeing them sent a shiver down Evan's spine. They were looking for him, or at least threats *like* him.

Evan tuned the other monitor to the live network coverage of the presidential debate. The show wouldn't start for another one hundred and fifty minutes, but the pundits were already discussing what they expected to see.

He switched on the webcam and the LED desk lamp, blinking in its harsh, white glow. He stared at his reversed image on the laptop screen. He looked exhausted, there were dark spots like bruises under his eyes. He hadn't shaved in days, didn't remember when he had last showered. His face shined with per-spiration.

He looked away. He didn't recognize himself.

Evan rubbed his hand over his face and pushed back his greasy hair. He hit Record and began the first of his video mes-sages.

"Hi, Allie, Tony. Mom and Dad. If you're watching this, then you know what I had to do. Remember that: *I had to do it*. You may know why by now, but you still won't understand it. And maybe you won't ever forgive me. . . ." He needed them to understand that they were better off, that he was doing this for them.

The second video began in much the same way. "Excelsior! Hey, P-Squared. I bet you want to kill me right now, huh?" He laughed. He glanced at his reflection, remembered to smile. Then he shook his head. She wouldn't care. She would under-stand. "I'm sorry," he said.

The third video he recorded was even harder. He imagined what Max would look like when he watched it, where he would be. Who he might be with.

He finished recording his messages and squirreled them away online. They would be delivered to his friends and family when it was time.

Time. It was almost four o'clock now, and he still had some preparations to make. There was a chance Infiltraitor would contact him before it was too late.

Evan dialed a number. He hated using his phone as a phone, but he needed to calm down, and there was only one person who could do that for him. But the line just rang and rang and rang.

Then she answered, and Evan sighed with relief.

"Hey," she said.

"Excelsior!" Evan said.

She laughed.

"I miss you, P-Squared," he said.

"Is something wrong, Ev?" she asked.

"Not right now." He closed his eyes and pictured her. "Right now, everything is perfect. Tell me about your day."

TUESDAY

7:15 A.M.

EVAN STUMBLED INTO THE KITCHEN and was surprised to see his parents still home.

"Good morning," Allie said. "Have some eggs."

Evan wrinkled his nose and went for his usual box of Cheerios.

"We're out of milk," Allie said.

"Don't need milk," Evan said.

"Aren't you going to be late for school?" Tony asked. He didn't look up from his tablet.

"No school. They closed it to set up for the debate tonight." Evan shoveled dry cereal into his mouth.

"That's right," Allie said. "You look terrible. Maybe you should skip it."

He nodded. Swallowed. "Good idea. I'll just watch it online."

"Honey, did you take your . . ."

Evan grunted. He took another bite of cereal and chewed.

His mother sighed. "Well, *I'm* going to be late for school," Allie said. She taught at ITT Tech. "Since we came back a day early, I offered to help out at the career fair today."

"I'll drop you off." Tony Baxter rose from the table, typing a message into his phone. "It's on the way to the office."

"We'll see you tonight, Evan. We can watch the debate on TV together. Max's girlfriend is going to be on, isn't she?"

"I guess so." Evan forced himself to look up at his mother. He got up and hugged her. She hid her surprise. "I love you," he said into her hair.

"I love you, too," Allie said. She looked at him for a long moment.

She knows, Evan thought. But she ruffled his hair and picked up her briefcase.

Evan nodded at Tony. "Have a good day."

"Thanks," his father said. "Feel better."

"Feel better" was as close as Tony would come to saying "I love you" to Evan.

As soon as his father's BMW pulled out of the driveway, Evan went back upstairs and got dressed, picking the cleanest black T-shirt and cargo pants from the pile of identical clothes on the floor of his closet. His mother criticized him for buying ten of everything and wearing the same thing every day, but he liked the idea of a uniform, and getting dressed was more efficient when he didn't have to worry about what to wear or what matched. He shrugged into his favorite red hoodie (he only had one, a gift from Max) and zipped it up.

Evan packed up his equipment while the drives on his other machines were being wiped. Finally, he went into the master bedroom and pried up the floorboard covering the secret compartment in the closet. He lifted out a heavy bundle and unwrapped the soft, greased cloth to reveal the black revolver, a Heckler and Koch USP 9. He loaded a magazine and checked the safety before stowing it in his backpack.

TUESDAY

4:51 P.M.

EVAN SAW MAX ON THE security camera in high-definition color as he walked through the auditorium behind Isaac Ramirez, one of his soccer teammates on the Granville Capybaras.

Evan could see everything: Max's girlfriend, Courtney Garcia, sat in front of the auditorium, just below the stage, which had been set up with a couple of podiums for the presidential candidates and a large video screen. The screen looked about fifty feet tall.

The lovebirds were both texting on their phones, probably to each other.

May I cut in? Evan thought.

He hit Send on the text message he had prepared for Max in LemonJuice, an encryption app Evan had designed himself.

hey, bud stop i need your help with this stop i know you'll figure out what to do with it stop good luck stop

a9 %_!;e3 Z_j*g29@X; aso] dr23\\8i #qWd|0?

It always pissed Max off when Evan used "stop" instead of a period, as if he were sending a message through the old telegraph system. Max called it an "affectation," but Evan's whole life was built around affectations.

He wiped his phone and switched it off. On the screen, Max lifted his head and looked around the auditorium.

"I'm right here." Evan waved to the screen.

He removed the battery of his phone and destroyed the SIM card for good measure. There would be no recovering data from it, no matter how good the government tech experts were. (They weren't very.) There was no turning back. If Infiltraitor didn't come through, he was going to have to see this to the end.

The presidential debate graphic billowed on the screen. Evan turned up the volume.

It was starting.

"Good evening from Granville High School in Granville, California. I'm Bennett Avery of *Newsroom* on *CNN*. I welcome you to our second presidential debate, between the Republican nominee, Senator Clancy Tooms, Jr. of Utah, and the Democratic nominee, Governor Angela S. Lovett of Tennessee."

Where are you, Infiltraitor?

"Throughout the debate, we will play pre-recorded video

27

messages asking questions of each of the candidates," Avery went on.

Evan opened another window to monitor the debate on Panjea; hundreds of thousands of people were live blogging about it on the social network. A message from Angela Lovett rolled across and was instantly Amplified: Hello, Granville HS! :) #webdeb

Evan had to hand it to Lovett and her media advisor Kevin Sharpe: They knew how to use social media to win people over.

"Our first question comes from Kennedy Richards. . . ."

Showtime.

TUESDAY

10:30 A.M.

EVAN SAT ON THE BLEACHERS facing the soccer field. Tomorrow afternoon it would be packed with students, teachers, and parents cheering on the Granville Capybaras in their soccer match against Monte Vida.

Still unable to reach Max, Evan had hoped to find his friend running the Granville High School track on his day off. No such luck.

He lifted his camera, focused it on the starting positions on the empty track, and snapped a photo. He carefully replaced the lens cap, slung the camera over one shoulder, and then headed for the main building.

The road in front of the high school was lined with black SUVs and news vans from every major network, with satellite dishes mounted on their roofs and miles of thick cables running alongside them. The dozens of cameras, reporters, and bright lights looked out of place on the school lawns.

Evan walked right past a large gray trailer emblazoned with the Panjea logo. A security detail guarded it; Evan suspected the server hosting video for tonight's broadcast was inside it.

There were more Secret Service agents posted at the school entrance. The debate didn't start for hours, and the building was strictly off-limits to nonessential personnel. Evan could work his way around most computer security precautions, but he had a much harder time tricking his way past people. Max had always been in charge of in-person infiltration attempts like this.

"Kid, look me in the eyes," the agent said.

Evan held up his camera, keeping his eyes down. "I'm covering the debate for the school blog. I need some shots of the setup."

"Please lower your voice and speak calmly," the agent said.

Evan bit his lip. He hadn't realized he was shouting.

"It's okay. He's with me," a girl said behind Evan.

He didn't need to turn around to recognize Courtney Garcia's voice. Whatever his issues with her, she had a beautiful voice. He had never heard her sing, and didn't even know if she could, but it still sounded like music to Evan.

"And who are *you* with?" the agent asked.

"Press." Courtney held up a badge. "I'm part of the program tonight. Courtney Garcia." It had been Courtney's winning student essay that had brought the national debate to Granville in the first place.

The agent checked a list on a clipboard. "All right. Go on through the metal detectors."

Once they were inside, Evan charged off on his own. The halls were packed like they were on any school day, but instead of students, he had to push his way through throngs of reporters and people in suits. They made him anxious.

"Evan. *You're welcome*," Courtney called.

Evan stopped short. "What?" he asked.

She caught up to him. "Kim Lee is the photographer assigned tonight. Also, you don't even work for the blog."

"Okay," Evan said.

"So what are you doing here?"

"There's a computer problem in the control booth. I volunteered to help." He looked around, hoping they wouldn't draw too much attention standing in the middle of a hallway.

"Why didn't you say so?" she asked.

"It was none of his business." Evan gritted his teeth.

"Evan. You don't have to look at my face, but please stop staring at my chest." She said it gently, and he revised his opinion of her slightly. She seemed to know he didn't mean anything by focusing there, but of course Max would have told her about Evan's Asperger's diagnosis. Still, people weren't often this patient and kind to him, and he knew how sensitive she was to that kind of attention.

"Sorry." Evan lifted his head, but he looked past her. Secret Service agents were escorting a group of reporters into the school's gymnasium. "Thank you."

He appreciated reminders to behave the way people expected. Over time, he had programmed himself to remember to say things like "sorry" and "thank you" because he knew they made other people feel better.

But Courtney probably thought he was thanking her for getting him inside the school. And he guessed that she wanted an explanation.

What if he told Courtney everything, before the debate? She could publish it all on her blog, Full Cort Press. For some reason, that conspiracy guy from Fawkes Rising had been following her posts lately, so it would be noticed, particularly with the eyes of the world on her and Granville High tonight. Courtney should be protected here, surrounded by federal agents.

But if even one of the government agents couldn't be trusted, this could also be the most dangerous place for her. Max would never forgive Evan if he got Courtney hurt, and Evan could never forgive himself for hurting Max.

Maybe he could tell another reporter here? Pick a press card, any press card.

That would be a great way to get himself noticed, and likely detained. He was grasping at straws. Giving this story to Courtney would be a cowardly way out, but it was a good backup to the backup plan. (Evan had tried talking to another reporter before, and that had gone poorly.) He pushed it to the back of his mind, filed it away for later, if there was a later.

"Evan?" Courtney asked. "Can I?"

"Yes?" He hadn't heard her question.

"Can I come with you? I'd like to see the control booth."

Evan's eyes darted down again, this time to focus on the Press badge pinned to the lapel of Courtney's jacket.

"Okay," he said.

He continued walking toward the auditorium at a brisk pace, unconcerned about whether she was keeping up. She hurried after him, her high heels on the tiles echoing like gunshots.

"Where have you been?" Courtney asked.

"Has someone been looking for me?" he asked. Panic crept into his voice.

"No. I don't think so." She sounded confused. "I just haven't seen you around much lately."

"Oh," he said.

After some time had passed, she sighed. Evan realized she probably had thought he was going to elaborate.

"I've been reading your blog. You're brave to stand up to the administration," he said.

"Thanks," she said. "I just feel like I have a responsibility, you know?"

"'A responsibility to the truth.'" He quoted her blog. "'Reporter first, high school student second.' I understand completely." Evan was a hacker before anything else.

They arrived at the auditorium and Evan let Courtney take over when they were questioned by a woman with a security earpiece coiled behind her ear. Courtney said Evan needed to get some shots for her article about the debate. They would just be a minute.

With the agent standing right outside, probably eavesdropping, Evan snapped a bunch of pictures and explained the controls for the lights and speakers to Courtney. He pointed out the computer that operated the video projection system. It was likely linked to the server in the trailer outside.

He pointed to the panel of LCD screens. "Those also monitor all the security feeds in the school."

The mosaic of images rotated through all the cameras in the school. Evan watched the federal agents move methodically from one camera to another, sweeping the school. The panel in the middle was frozen on the auditorium, a wide angle that gave a high-definition view of the stage and the screen set up on it. Right now, the expansive room was swarming with a security team checking under every seat.

While Courtney was distracted by the action on the screens, Evan flipped open a compartment on his camera and popped out the SD card. He inserted it into a slot on the back of the computer and then unplugged it. When he powered it back up, it would read the card and run a script that would give him access not only to the contents of the hard drive, but allow him to patch into the live video feed later tonight—right through the firewall and the additional layers of security added for the debate.

Evan watched Courtney for a moment. "Those cameras are always recording," he said carefully. "Security footage is archived on a separate server for thirty days."

She nodded.

"What the hell?" A voice barked from behind them. Evan turned and clenched his fists in his pant pockets when he saw the man in the gray turtleneck with a tablet computer tucked under one arm. "No one is supposed to be in here."

"I'm Courtney Garcia." Courtney smiled and extended a hand. The man glanced down at her press badge. "Do you have time for an interview?"

"An interview?" The man looked startled.

"You're Kevin Sharpe," Evan said. He had never seen the man in person, but he recognized him instantly from his photos in the tech magazines that had been featuring him regularly in the past year.

"Yes, I am. And you are?" Sharpe asked.

"I was asked to help fix this computer."

Evan looked behind the computer tower. "Here's the problem. It's unplugged." He reached down and plugged back in the cable he had pulled out. The machine whirred to life and the lights on the front flickered.

Dit dit dit. Dah dah dah. Dit dit dit.

Sharpe scrutinized Courtney.

Courtney's face flushed. "I'm a reporter for the school blog, and I also run my own blog."

"Oh, you're the kid *blogger*." Then Sharpe snapped his fingers. "That was a great essay you wrote. Tell you what, I'm not available for an interview, but I may be able to get you a few minutes with Governor Lovett later. How would you like that?"

"That would be *amazing*," Courtney said.

While they worked out the details, Evan surreptitiously popped the SD card out of the computer and put it back into his camera. He snapped a picture and the flash went off.

"Come find me after the debate, Ms. Garcia," Sharpe said. "But for now, you and your friend need to stay out of our way."

As they left, Evan saw Sharpe head straight for the server he had just compromised. He hoped the so-called "Architect" of Lovett's presidential campaign wasn't as good with computers as his reputation suggested.

"Oh my God! I could do a cartwheel right now!" Courtney looked down at her pantsuit and high heels. "Better not."

Her phone dinged. She checked it. "It's Max."

Evan hurried away. He had a few more errands to run, and he didn't have much time left.

TUESDAY

9:20 P.M.

EVAN COULDN'T WAIT FOR INFILTRAITOR any longer.

The debate was almost over. Evan grabbed Audrey II, the laptop he reserved for coding while offline, and carried it through the abandoned store. He had put this off until the last possible moment to make sure the data it contained made itself available only to someone who would put it to good use.

He jumped at every sound in the alley as he uploaded the files to the USB drive hidden by the store's entrance. He was nervous just standing there, exposed, when he was so close to the end. (The end of his part in this, anyway.)

He peered around the dimly lit lot. There were a few empty parked cars, which presumably belonged to the customers and staff of the coffee shop next door. He could be surrounded by FBI, for all he knew. They would be waiting for him to do something really incriminating, like hack into the presidential debate. There could be other people too, coming after his code.

Evan ducked back into the store. By the time he sat back down at the table, he had wiped all the contents of the laptop.

"Good night, Audrey."

He slipped the dead machine reverently into his backpack and pulled out his father's pistol. He loaded a clip and deposited the gun beside the mask on his table with a heavy, hollow *thud*.

Evan started streaming video from his webcam, for the moment broadcasting to no one but himself.

The video window showed his face in reverse. The frightened boy looking back at him was a stranger. He slipped on his white mask, right over his glasses. He was blind without them, and he needed to see everything clearly now.

There I am, he thought. *That's better.*

He pulled up his hood and took a deep breath.

"Hello, I'm Dramatis Personai," he said. The filter inside his mask gave him a synthetic, mechanical voice.

He opened the chat window and saw messages from the other members of his group wondering about the big, mysterious stunt he had been promising for the debate.

Evan silently mouthed the group's signature greeting: *Life is theater.*

A private message popped up. Evan groaned.

DoubleThink>>STOP: I looked up the first telegraph message you're always talking about.

Sent by Samuel F.B. Morse on May 23, 1844, to his assistant

Alfred Vail, the first telegraph message read, "What hath God wrought?"

Watch.

Evan looked at the feed from the debate. They were on the next-to-last question. Tooms went first.

Laugh.

DoubleThink>>STOP: Did you know the phrase was chosen by a teenage girl?

Of course he knew that. Her name was Annie Ellsworth.

DoubleThink>>STOP: Her name was Annie Ellsworth. Cool, huh?

Annie's mother had actually selected the quote from the *Book of Numbers*, from the pleasingly symmetrical line 23:23.

"For there is no enchantment against Jacob, no divination against Israel, now it shall be said of Jacob and Israel, 'What hath God wrought!'"

Weep.

The inside of Evan's mask was wet with tears and sweat. His vision was blurring, his glasses were slipping. (Emotions are so inconvenient.) He licked his lips under his mask.

Now Governor Lovett was halfway through her response. One minute left.

STOP>>DoubleThink: I have to go.

He didn't want to go. He had so much more to say.

Evan signed off and set his self-destruct sequence to erase Rorschach's hard drive three minutes from now, unless he stopped it.

Evan's right knee knocked against the bottom of the table. *Dit dit dit. Dah dah dah. Dit dit dit.*

SOS. Send Help.

Jack Phillips had sent that signal as the *Titanic* sank, right up until the ship's wireless room flooded. He made it to an overturned lifeboat, but he died in the frigid Atlantic waters, waiting for someone to save him. He gave his life to summon help for the other passengers and crew.

Evan stilled his leg. It was time to send *his* distress call.

On Evan's second monitor, Bennett Avery said, "Our last video question comes from Samir Gupta in Bakersfield, California."

Evan muted the program and seized control of the video feed. He cut off the official video link and the screen filled with a colorful array of shifting pixels. "Sorry, Samir," he said. Whatever Samir's question might be, Evan had a much more important one to ask.

The curtain is rising.

He linked his own camera into the video feed, then looked straight into the lens.

"Hello?" His disguised voice was cold, flat, and ugly.

Evan thought he heard a sound deep in the store and turned his head to the right. He listened. It could have been a rat knocking over trash, or a loose board being lifted and dropped. Or someone coming for him. Or his imagination.

He had to hurry. He turned back to the camera and breathed in and out. "My name is STOP."

On screen, the closed captioning showed Avery responding with "What's going on?"

"Do you really want to know?" Evan asked. "Just listen. *Listen.*"

He pressed the macro key on his keyboard.

"I have a question. What is the silence of six, and what are you going to do about it?" he asked.

Blood rushed to Evan's ears, making it difficult to hear. Were those footsteps? Or just his own heartbeat pounding in his head? He couldn't turn to look for intruders in the darkness, if they were there. If they were closing in. Anyway, it was too late.

Evan fought the urge to blurt out everything now, all the horrors he had learned (and inspired) in the last year—but there just wasn't time. There wasn't time. There wasn't time.

Dit. Dit. Dit.

And no one would believe him if he did. The truth had to come out when the moment was right, from the right people. Not him.

And he could finally protect those people for once, with a sacrifice for a sacrifice. Six of one, half a dozen of another.

(Was there someone there?)

He straightened in his chair and pulled back his hood. He lifted his mask with one hand and lifted the gun with the other.

(They were closing in.)

"I'm sorry, I'm sorry, I'm sorry," he muttered. His own voice sounded naked and lonely in the hopefully empty store.

Dah. Dah. Dah.

They couldn't ignore Evan any longer. They couldn't ignore the truth. They couldn't ignore the horrors unfolding right in front of them. This message was finally the one thing that they would never be able to hide.

(They were in his head.)

Dit.

He would do this for his mom and dad, for P-Squared, for Max. For Ariel and Infiltraitor and Kyle, and the others. And for at least two hundred million people he'd never meet, nor never would.

You're welcome.

Dit.

He thumbed off the safety, ready to go out fighting.

(This is how he would get into *their* heads.)

Dit.

DOUBLETHINK

UMPQUA COMMUNITY COLLEGE
ROSEBURG, OR

SEPT. 15, 11:34 A.M.

PENNY POLONSKY TRIED, AND FAILED, to stifle a yawn while Professor Saroyan droned on at the front of the class-room. She was tired, essentially running on root beer Bawls, but she was more bored than anything else. She could pass this Orientation to Programming class, the first step to earning an Associate of Applied Science degree she didn't particularly want, in her sleep—and she probably would, the way things were going.

Penny yawned again. She'd been up late again testing the online security of her newest client, Lectric Motors. It had only taken a month of sleepless nights to get into their systems, but other than some mundane corporate emails and outdated sche-matics, she hadn't found anything juicy—and her contract was almost up.

From her employer's perspective, that was a good thing; they didn't want hackers like her to be able to break into their servers and steal information on their new products. That's why they had hired her, or more accurately her alter ego Emmie Steed, to do her best to do the worst. Regardless of how far she made it, she would collect a check, but there would be more zeroes at the end of it, not to mention bragging rights, if she managed to break into a sensitive area.

Of course, she cared more about her reputation. Not being able to p0wn the company—any company—made her feel like a failure.

Penny was feeling like a failure a lot lately: as a daughter, a sister, a student, a girlfriend. She hadn't been able to connect with anyone IRL the way she could online. Computers were so much easier than people! The only thing that she was good at was hacking, and she still wasn't the best. She wasn't even the best one living in her house.

And here she was at college, just going through the motions. Too bad she couldn't get credit for all her former exploits in Dramatis Personai.

The look on Saroyan's face if he saw what she could really do with a computer would be priceless, but it would also confirm his suspicions of her. The next thing she knew, she'd be hearing heavy knocks on her bedroom door, and then she'd be dragged away from her house in a black car. She'd avoided that fate so far, and she was determined to keep it that way.

Penny opened one of her unencrypted email accounts and

idly scrolled through the messages. She hadn't checked this one in a while, and spam had taken over most of the inbox like weeds choking an untended garden. However, one email made her sit up, now wide awake: a news alert she had set to crawl the web for specific terms. There was a new match for "Gyaraga 1981," an online puzzle that appeared each September to challenge obsessive fans of alternate-reality games.

Penny had almost forgotten all about it, but the game was back again, like clockwork. Her friend Evan had always been fascinated with ARGs, like the ones movie studios made to promote new movies and video games, and he had participated in Gyaraga 1981 every year, without fail. But since he had had died last October, Penny was planning to do it in his memory. She was going to win this one for him.

No one knew what happened when you reached the end. Some people thought the NSA or another "intelligence" agency was using it as a recruitment tool for creative thinkers and hackers. Participants usually pooled their knowledge in Reddit forums to figure out the answers to more difficult and esoteric puzzles, so only the people who reached the goal fastest—most likely on their own—were contacted by the game organizers, whoever they were.

Penny opened an encrypted browser and clicked the link to the IP address provided in her search results: 24.132.231.42, noting the elegant symmetry. Evan would have appreciated that. A webpage loaded with painstaking slowness, ultimately revealing blocky red numbers and letters that read: 23:26:10.

The number was going backward, decreasing a second at a time.

A countdown, in hours, minutes, and seconds. She apparently had twenty-four hours, until . . . what?

Electronic piano music blared from her speakers.

"Shit!" Penny fumbled the mouse and muted her laptop quickly. But it was too late. The sound had echoed through the lecture room and briefly drowned out Professor Saroyan, who was now staring at her—along with everyone else.

"Ms. Polonsky, am I boring you?" Saroyan called from the front of the room.

A few people chuckled.

"No, Professor. I'm sorry about that." The worst thing was, she deserved his mockery—this time.

Who the hell embeds music on autoplay in 2015?

"I know you're friends with a world-famous hacktivist." Saroyan didn't even attempt to hide his disdain for the term. He'd let Penny, and the rest of the students know, what little regard he had for hackers, no matter what color their hat.

She thought there was some professional jealousy lurking behind the massive chip on his shoulder, but that didn't do her any good. So she tried to keep a low profile, the way she always had until the Panjea incident had put Max Stein and her in the headlines. He'd gotten the worst of it, which helped keep Penny's own hacking history a secret, but part of her bristled at being cast as the stereotypical damsel in distress.

Somehow it seemed worse now that she and Max were a

thing. Like she was a prize, a princess he'd found in a castle. Penny was no princess.

Saroyan was still talking. What did he just say? "—and if you don't listen, you'll have a hard time keeping up. This is the most basic of basic computer science," he said.

No kidding, Penny thought.

"It gets much harder from here. We can't afford to waste each other's time," he continued.

Penny gritted her teeth. Her mild embarrassment quickly transitioned to anger. He had that tone, the one he only seemed to use for her and the other eleven women in a class of more than a hundred students. No, make that ten women. Lily had dropped it yesterday.

"Yes, sir." Penny pointed at the screen behind the professor. He liked to walk around the front of the room, flashing slides around importantly like he was doing his own personal TED talk. But he wasn't helping to change the world with new ideas, he was only demonstrating how stuck the world was in its old ones.

"But . . . you're missing a line there?" Penny instantly hated the way that question mark had slipped in when she knew this stuff better than anyone in the room. She set her jaw and spoke clearly, confidently. "It's best practice to check that the user's input is valid so the program doesn't enter an infinite loop."

So basic.

"Oh, I think you'll see that I already . . ." Professor Saroyan looked down at his own computer screen. He was quiet for a long moment. "Ah, you have been paying attention! Clever girl!" He quickly added the missing data line. "But I would appreciate it if there were no more distractions," he added brusquely before returning to his lesson.

Clever girl. Clever girl. Clever girl.

She looked around the classroom and saw a sea of people surfing on Panjea instead of paying attention. She couldn't believe people still trusted Panjea. After everything she and her friends had gone through last year, they had barely made a dent in the company's image. They certainly hadn't managed to change the public's online behavior. Even if Panjea's new CEO, Gwendolyn Dixon, was true to her word and the company was now strictly legal, there were plenty of other ways for your information to be compromised. The more you put out there, the more power you gave others.

I'll show you who's clever, Penny thought. In a couple of minutes she could redirect everyone's computers to porn sites, including the good professor's.

The boy next to her leaned closer. "What an ass," he said.

Penny turned to him, her face turning red. "What did you say?"

The boy faltered. "Saroyan. He's an ass. He wasted more of our time calling you out for an honest mistake than if he'd just ignored it and kept teaching." He smiled. "You're Peggy, right?"

"Close enough," she muttered.

"Huh?"

"That's right," she said.

"Hey, how did you know that? About the mistake in his code. I still don't follow what it's supposed to do."

"Gosh, it must have been a lucky guess," Penny said.

"That's what I thought." He smiled. "I'm Malcolm. Mal."

"'*Mal*' means 'bad' in Spanish. Did you know that?"

"No, but that's . . . interesting. Nice nail polish. What's it say?"

Penny held up her hands, palms facing her.

He looked at the words painted on the nails of her fingers and thumbs in large, friendly letters and frowned. His lips moved as he sounded each one out. Jesus, he couldn't read.

"D-O-N-apostrophe-T-P-A-N-I-C," she said.

"Don . . . T . . . ?"

"Don't panic!" she snapped. *He can't even spell?*

"Oh!" He nodded. "Good advice. Ooh, is that a video game?" He stared at Penny's screen, which still displayed the countdown, now at 23:23:02. Speaking of wasting time. One more reason her classes were getting in the way of what she'd rather be doing with her life.

"No." She hit ALT-TAB to switch back to the class assignment, which she had finished thirty minutes earlier. Screw it. She checked to make sure she'd included a couple of wrong answers so Professor Saroyan wouldn't accuse her of cheating again and submitted it early.

"Okay," Malcolm said. "You know, after class, how about we—"

"No," Penny said.

"Coffee?"

"Can't. Busy."

"Come on. Look, I think you're great. After Saroyan mentioned it, I read about what happened to you last year, that stuff with Panjea. It sounded scary. I'd like to hear more about it."

Penny sighed. "I have a boyfriend."

"Oh. Of course you do. Sorry." He mimed smacking himself in the forehead. "But I still think you're interesting." Malcolm turned back to his own computer.

She almost felt guilty, but by the time she looked down at the now-silent timer in her Tor browser, she had already pushed him out of her mind. She started counting down the minutes until classes were over for the day and she could start to figure this out.

THE POLONSKY RESIDENCE — ROSEBURG, OR

SEPT. 15, 03:04 P.M.

AFTER HER LAST CLASS OF the day, Penny hurried back home for her regularly scheduled but increasingly irregular video chat with Max. He was now nine hours ahead of her, doing the first semester of his senior year of high school in Paris, and they'd been having trouble adjusting to the new schedule.

They were already used to the long-distance thing—Oregon to France wasn't that different from Oregon to California, in internet terms. And they both kept such weird hours, the time difference wasn't a big deal. The difficulty was . . . everything else.

It was hit or miss whether Max would even show up. He was often out and away from his computer, trying to track down leads on his absent mother's whereabouts. He was also spending more and more time with his new friends in Paris. The farther he pulled away from his online life, the farther he seemed to get from Penny as well.

This was how his friendship with Evan had fallen apart in the months before he'd died. You'd think Max would have learned his lesson. Penny had. She was trying to figure out if she should end things with Max before he faded on her, and if she did, should she do it while they were apart or wait until he got back to face him in person? Maybe when he came home at Christmas things would go back to normal for them.

Meanwhile, Penny continued to be on her computer as much as possible. Community college had ended up being as dull as she had feared. She still encountered the best challenges and the most interesting people online. The real world simply couldn't compare.

Maybe it would be different if she'd gone away for school. Not like another country, but leaving Oregon would have been nice. Hell, leaving home would make a world of difference. But then who would keep an eye on Risse? Penny had practically raised her younger sister while their mother was out working and spending the little money she earned gambling and drinking. Penny wasn't going to abandon Risse like their father had, no matter how much she wanted to leave.

Max wasn't signed in. Typical. Back to Gyaraga 1981.

Penny flopped onto her bed and loaded the countdown page on her laptop.

19:56:47

She wondered if she was meant to do something before time ran out, or if she was supposed to wait for something to happen in less than a day. That song might give her some indication.

She cranked up the volume on her shitty laptop speakers and listened to the tune. It was a MIDI version of a piano arrangement she had never heard before. Kind of catchy. DA DI DA DI DA DA DI DA. DA DI DA DI DA DA DI DA.

She listened to the whole thing once, then stopped it when it looped back to the beginning. She grabbed her phone and opened a music-recognition app, then played the music again, watching the waveform of the song as it played.

Thirty seconds later, the app found a match: "'Communications'—Slim Gaillard Trio, 1947," she read.

She searched for the song on her laptop and quickly found one of several YouTube videos with the song. "Thank you, internet," she said. She hit Play.

It was catchy. She found herself nodding her head and tapping her nails on her laptop in time with the beat. True to its refrain, "That's communication," Slim was singing about different ways of talking to people: telephone, microphone, Dictaphone, telegram, teletype, and so on. Evan so would have loved this.

The screen blurred. She blinked a couple of times and wiped the back of her hand across her eyes.

It's not fair. Evan should be here for this. Right now, he'd be sending her excited chat messages about the game. When he was working out a puzzle, he would send her a rapid-fire succession of messages—*ding ding ding ding*—more stream of consciousness than complete sentences. It was an interesting look into how his brain worked. He really did think that fast. He probably would have solved this clue already.

She checked her chat window. *Max, where are you?*

She sighed. Even if he'd been online, she couldn't tell him about this. For a while, it seemed like the main thing they shared was the pain they felt at Evan's absence. Neither of them could quite replace him in the other's life, especially once they had started talking around Evan, as though that would help them move on. But Penny clearly wasn't ready to move on, or she wouldn't be competing in this game right now. Maybe winning it would get her the closure she needed.

Penny played the song again. And again. Again.

She looked up when Risse came into her room and dropped her purple backpack on the floor.

"Nice tune. What is it?" Risse asked.

"You tell me," Penny said. She restarted the song and played the opening.

Da di da di da da di da.
Da di da di da da di da.
Da di da di da da di da.
Da di dit dit.

"The scatting . . ." Risse's eyes widened. "It's—"

"Morse code," Penny said. "I know!" She jumped up from her bed, clutching her laptop with both hands.

"Heart!" Risse said. "Where'd it come from?"

Penny paused. "Just something I stumbled across today."

"It's dash-dot-dash-dot dash-dash-dot-dash," Risse said. "That spells 'C-Q' three times."

Penny knew Morse code too; this was one of the best known signals out there, even more common than SOS.

"More or less. CQ is short for the French word '*sécurité*,' which translates as 'pay attention,'" she said. It certainly had her attention. "It was used as a distress call before SOS became popular, but ham radio operators still use it as an open call to anyone who wants to talk. The dash-dot-dot dot at the end is DE."

"That's French too?"

"Yup. The word for 'from.'"

"So what does it mean? Really mean?"

"I have no idea!" Penny smiled.

The music playing on her computer blended with the jingle of an incoming video call.

"There's my cue to go. Tell Max I say hi." Risse scooped up her bag and headed for the door. Penny settled back down on her bed.

She paused the music and accepted Max's video call. She peeled the tape away from her webcam. A moment later, Max's face appeared in her chat window. She could only tell it was him from his mess of dark hair—the picture quality was badly degraded, pixels sliding around like one of those tile puzzles she'd played with as a kid.

"Hey, sorry I'm late. I just got in," Max said.

"Isn't it after midnight there?" Penny asked.

"Yeah. I lost track of the time. Enzo's teaching me how to pick pockets."

Penny raised an eyebrow. "Oh?" she said, in case her image was as wacky on his end.

"What are you up to?" he asked.

"Research."

"A new job?" Max asked.

"Sort of an old one, for a friend."

He nodded. At least, it looked like he did. His mouth swapped places with his eyes for a moment, pieces of his face breaking down into seemingly random noise.

"We have a terrible connection," she said.

"I know. I'm trying to get my host family to switch to a better provider. But it's kind of a mixed blessing, since it keeps me off my computer more. Aside from seeing you, I don't need to be online much anyway these days."

Penny shuddered. "That's like saying you don't need air."

"You don't think I'd look good bald?" Max asked.

"I said *air*. Not *hair*. But bald men are kind of sexy."

"Duly noted. How was your day?" Even with the bad connection, she could hear the tentativeness in his voice.

"Oh, Max. I still hate it," Penny said.

"Do you hate college, or do you hate living at home?" Max said.

Penny narrowed her eyes. "You're too good at figuring people out."

"*Other* people. Penny, what do you—?"

"What?" she asked.

Max sighed. "Never mind. Just, give it more time. You've only been in class a few weeks. You can do this. You can do anything you want."

"Thanks. I think that might be my problem. Hey, so you're learning to pick pockets?" she asked, trying to shift the subject.

"No. I said my host brother's teaching me. Trying to, that is."

"And here I thought you were on the straight and narrow. Any luck searching for your mom?"

Max's face fell. Literally, in a rain of mismatched blocks of color.

"No. There's still no sign of her online." Penny heard the disappointment in his voice. If she could have, she would have reached out for Max's hand and squeezed it. There were some drawbacks to interacting through a computer screen after all.

Penny knew exactly what Max was feeling. She'd given up on finding her own father years ago, after drawing a similar blank in her online searches. Now if she discovered he was in Europe, or even somewhere else in Oregon, she didn't think she'd bother traveling there to meet him. She'd come to believe she and Risse were better off without their father, if he didn't want to be with them. Today, his disappearance only bothered her the way any unsolved puzzle would.

But Max wanted to find Lianna Stein so much, Penny really wanted him to succeed.

"You don't need to be in France to find her," Penny said.

Max sighed in frustration. "We've been over this. You can't do everything from behind a keyboard."

"Pffpt. Maybe *you* can't." Penny forced a jokey tone to lighten the mood. She didn't want to waste another video call arguing with Max.

"I'm serious. I've been investigating political activist groups, poring through old newspapers and court records," Max said. "Mom used to be into that stuff when she was with Dad, so I figure . . . well, you don't give that sort of thing up, do you?"

"Your father did," Penny said. *You did*, she almost added.

Max yawned loudly. The image froze with his mouth comically wide open.

"Hello?" Penny asked.

"Yeah. Um, can you see me?"

"You stopped moving."

Max groaned.

"Forget it. You're tired, Max. Let's try this again tomorrow night." She switched her browser over to the ticking clock on the countdown. "And I still have some time-sensitive work to do."

"Okay. Good night, Pen."

You agreed with me way too quickly, she thought. *For once.*

"Good night. Oh, wait. Hey, have you ever heard a song called 'Communications' by Slim Gaillard?"

"Hmmm . . . Yeah. Once. It was on one of Evan's playlists. Not really my thing. Why?"

Max was skilled at the art of deception, but she didn't think he was lying to her. He wasn't playing Gyaraga 1981—he probably wouldn't even be interested, given how far removed his life had become from her world of hackers.

"No reason. Talk to you later."

THE SAME ROOM PENNY HAS LIVED IN FOR 18 YEARS — ROSEBURG, OR

SEPT. 16, 04:34 A.M.

"YOU'RE STILL UP?" RISSE SAID from the bedroom door.

Penny paused the video she was watching and spun her chair to face her younger sister. "No. You're dreaming. And sleepwalking."

"Ha." Risse yawned and slipped inside the room, casting a worried backward glance to Mama's room at the end of the hall. She sat on the bed, folded her legs under her comfortably, and then glanced at Penny's screen. If it had been anyone but her, Penny would have been annoyed. Her work was private. But she never kept secrets from Risse.

Penny was unhappy living at home, but she would have been unhappier living without Risse. As long as she needed Penny, Penny would be here for her. Besides, it was like missing half her brain when they were apart.

"Watching a movie?" Risse asked.

"It's called *CQ*," Penny said.

"Like that Morse code song from before." Risse gave Penny a look that said she knew she was holding back. "You want my help with whatever this is?"

"Not unless you want to make me some popcorn." She appreciated the offer, but this was something she wanted to do on her own.

"I'll pass." Risse yawned again and got up.

"Why are *you* up so late?" Penny asked.

"DP," Risse said.

Dramatis Personai. Risse was spending more and more time in their chat rooms, as her online identity, DoubleThink. Once Penny had taken an extended leave from the hacking collective, Risse took over their handle and the unofficial job of keeping the guys in line.

"They're still excited about Ada Kiesler?" Penny asked.

Kiesler was the latest whistleblower to make headlines. She had leaked emails exposing criminal activity at the German media giant Verbunden Telekom—or tried to. Her files had mysteriously disappeared as quickly as she'd posted them, and no reputable news source would work with her. She had gone into hiding at some embassy in Berlin.

"Everyone wants to help her, but so far all we can come up with is doxxing execs at VT. That's not how we do things anymore. Not on my watch," Risse said.

Penny paused and studied Risse. Long rumpled hair, one

braid coming apart, purple unicorn pajamas. She was both really young and incredibly mature at the same time. How many girls had changed the world before their fifteenth birthday?

Probably more than you ever hear about.

Penny was proud of her sister, but she couldn't resist. "Be careful. Lots of surveillance around this one."

"Lots of surveillance around *everything*. That's the point." Risse rubbed her eyes. "Anyway, I have a math test in a few hours, so good night."

"I don't know how you do it all," Penny said.

"I don't get enough sleep." Risse hugged Penny from behind. "But you should."

"Soon. G'night, Risse."

Her sister left and closed the door behind her.

Penny had less than seven hours left on the clock. She could wait it out and see what happened when it reached zero—but that could kick her out of the running.

"What am I supposed to do?" Penny said aloud to the closed door.

She finished watching the movie while she mulled over her options. *CQ* was pretty damn weird but not very enlightening; she hadn't found anything that seemed connected to the characters and references in the movie. Now she was struggling to keep her eyes open. She reloaded the YouTube video of Gaillard's "Communications," popped in her earbuds, and listened to the song again. She fell asleep before the short song ended.

She snapped awake four hours later. The song was still playing on loop: "When you send this way, how much time you save?"

Penny slumped forward and rubbed her eyes. She'd had an idea. She looked at all the audio recordings of the song on YouTube. There were four. One of them, not the one she'd been listening to, had only been uploaded two days ago. That was a hell of a coincidence, unless it wasn't.

She listened to that video, but as far as she could tell, it was identical to the one she'd already heard. She stopped it before it ended and scrolled through the information about the user who had shared it: pixel_prefect.

There was an email address on the account, hidden behind a CAPTCHA—which ended up being the trickiest test yet. She failed it three times, until she started wondering if maybe she was a robot after all and didn't know it. But she finally got it to work, more out of luck than anything, and the email address appeared: Class-O-81@freemail.net.

"Gotcha," she said.

But no, it was the opposite. *They've got me*, Penny thought. But what to write?

She finally settled on a line from that movie, *CQ*: "So this is the end . . . or is it the start? Of what?"

The email reply came back so fast, it had to be from an autoresponder: "First!" written in bright green, blinking, Comic fucking Sans MS. Beneath it was a strange icon, a circle over a caret, which looked familiar, though she couldn't place it.

o
∧

"What the crap?" she muttered.

Was she actually the first person to get this clue? Or did the message have some double meaning? Given the way these things went, she was betting on the latter.

A quick image search online revealed that the symbol was from the movie *Stargate*. Or one of the TV series, of which, apparently, there were many. Too many. It was an Egyptianish glyph that represented Earth.

Stargate. Okay. So what did "First!" mean?

What if only the first person to find the solution would move on to the next stage? Anyone could be competing with Penny, so she didn't want to reach out to Dramatis Personai for help and give the clue away. What about Risse? Or Max? If they weren't playing the game themselves, winning it would be a whole lot easier with their help.

No. Evan never asked me for help. He'd liked reasoning things out with her over chat, but only to have someone to talk to. He had never expected her to offer assistance, and she had known him well enough to realize he would have been offended if she'd tried. Reaching out to others for help was difficult for him, which was likely one of the reasons he'd ended up dead.

This isn't the same thing. This is only a game, Penny thought.

I can do this on my own.

She started opening multiple tabs in her browser and pulling information about ARGs. Arguably one of the first and most influential games was *The Beast* in 2001. She remembered Evan gushing about it in an online chat once, about how he wished he could have played it—although at the time he was still in diapers. She had heard of some of the other games too: *I Love Bees, lonelygirl15, Cathy's Book, Cloverfield.*

First. First. First . . .

She was really too tired for this right now. But if she was still racing against a clock, she couldn't stop now.

WOULDN'T YOU LIKE TO KNOW?
= ROSEBURG, OR

SEPT. 18, 10:21 P.M.

OVER THE PAST COUPLE OF days, Penny had watched the movie *Stargate* (terrible) the first season of the TV series (not bad), and several episodes from some of the other shows (why?). She read as much as she could about the sprawling franchise, and finally, she found another detail that seemed strikingly relevant:

Stargate was the first film to have its own marketing website.

The countdown clock had long since expired, taking the musical clue along with it. Anyone who hadn't found the site right away and gotten past that first hurdle was out of luck. The page had been replaced with a roster of the people who were still in the game, like the leader boards for top-scoring players on an old arcade game. They were identified only by their email addresses, perhaps to egg them on or foster competition. There was Penny's, at number 7 of 53: p-------d@freemail.net. Evan had nicknamed her "P-squared," and that was the account she had emailed him from the most.

Ping. A message popped up on her screen. It was still strange to see a message from DoubleThink—she had *been* DoubleThink before. Half of the two-person alias, anyway. But now it was all Risse. Who was sitting literally on the other side of Penny's bedroom wall.

They messaged each other all the time, even when they were in the same room, and especially late at night when they didn't want to wake their mother or stop their respective work to have a conversation.

DoubleThink: Hey.

+g00d: Hey. Is everything okay?

DoubleThink: Everything's fine. Great, actually. I, um, have a date?

+g00d: WHAT.

Penny paused in her search for the original *Stargate* website.

DoubleThink: Right?

+g00d: Who is he? She? They?

DoubleThink: Emerson Swift.

Penny vaguely remembered a Todd Swift in her class. She didn't pay attention to a lot of real-world stuff, like *people*, but she thought Todd was decent looking. She distinctly remembered that he had hair and eyes, and a mouth. Probably a nose too, but she couldn't swear on it.

She looked Todd up on Panjea; she still kept her Emmie Steed account there, the better to manipulate dudes in the tech industry.

Oh, okay. That guy. Yup. He did have a nose, just like she'd thought. And freckles. The very definition of unmemorable.

His younger brother, Emerson, did not have a Panjea account, or any online presence she could see. So that was promising.

+g00d: How did this happen?

DoubleThink: He asked me out at lunch. I said "No." He said, "That's disappointing, but I understand. I hope we can be friends." And I said, "Can I change my answer?"

+g00d: OMG. I would ask whether he has an older brother, but . . .

DoubleThink: You have Max. Don't be greedy. And Emerson's definitely the cuter brother.

+g00d: Verified. So where's he taking you?

DoubleThink: He thought I might be interested in the "mythical creatures" exhibit at the Douglas County Natural History Museum.

+g00d: Perfect. It's almost like he knows you!

DoubleThink: He said it took him a year to work up the courage to ask me out. And . . .

+g00d: What?

DoubleThink: He wanted to wait until you had graduated and moved far away. :-P

+g00d: And he's smart too. That's amazing, honey. But

please tell him I'm still living at home. And our walls are paper thin.

Penny heard Risse mumble something from her room. She took a guess.

+good: Yes they are.

DoubleThink: !!!

+good: PAPER THIN.

How does Risse do it? Somehow, she managed to have it all. She was a brilliant hacker, a good student, participated in clubs and stuff, and she actually had a social life. Maybe a boyfriend soon.

God. Maybe sex.

Okay, stop that thought right there.

Somehow people like Risse and Max were able to have real-life friendships in the physical world. They went out and did things, just for fun. Because they had nothing better to do. Instead, Penny lived for puzzles and hacking and making a difference, and that didn't leave much room for anything else. Or she *wouldn't* make room for it, the way Risse did. Risse could lead the life of both a "normal" teenager and a hacktivist, instead of having to choose one or the other, one of the many conflicts Penny and Max had been struggling with lately. Maybe they should ask Risse for some couples counseling.

DoubleThink: Really, what have you been up to? You've barely left your room for days. Have you even been going to class?

+g00d: Erm, no. I've been busy.

DoubleThink: Doing what?

+g00d: I've been . . . watching, uh . . . *Stargate.*

There was a long pause. Penny chewed on a fingernail.

Is Risse competing with me? She scanned the list of other players. She saw email addresses that could be for some of the lesser hackers she knew from DP, but nothing she immediately associated with her sister, or Max. Not that creating a dummy email address was difficult at all.

DoubleThink: Um. Who are you, and what have you done with my sister?

Penny sighed in relief. Risse had probably just been multi-tasking, carrying on other conversations at the same time.

Or she was playing it cool and doing a better job of hiding the fact that she was in this thing too. She couldn't recall Risse ever showing an interest in Gyaraga 1981 before. Penny was just overly paranoid, an instinct the events of the last year had only made worse.

Risse wouldn't keep it from her anyway. Realizing that made Penny feel even guiltier for shutting her out.

+g00d: It's for a job. I think. Sort of. Just something I'm working on pro bono.

DoubleThink: This is related to that Morse code song? Why are you being like this?

+g00d: Like what?

DoubleThink: Like, secret agency. Don't make me come in there.

+g00d: I'll tell you when I know this all isn't a waste of my time. So I don't waste any of yours.

DoubleThink: :-/

Penny continued researching online while they chatted, often with long stretches between replies. Risse said that Dramatis Personai was zeroing in on a new target of interest, but she couldn't say who. She apologized, but Penny said that was the choice she'd made when she separated from the group.

It seemed like they both had their secrets these days. One more sign of what Penny had walked away from when she left DP.

Penny finally dug up the URL for the original *Stargate* website in an old newsgroup. She typed in the address http://www.digiplanet.com/STARGATE, not expecting anything to be there after more than twenty years.

Surprise!

An image loaded showing a blocky but recognizable character from the 1980s: E.T. with the words "E.T. PHONE HOME!" The pixelated 8-bit alien seemed to have a gaping chest wound that he was trying to plug with a bloody finger, suggesting that he should try calling 911 instead.

The bottom of the image said "Copyright 1983 Atari, Inc. All Rights Reserved."

This appeared to be the title screen of that infamous video game of which Atari had buried millions of copies in a landfill.

Except no. When Penny looked it up, it was actually a *different* E.T. video game made the following year.

"Seriously?" Penny said. "Atari made a *sequel* to the worst video game in history?" Talk about gluttons for punishment. They had seemed intent on burying the entire video game industry.

She sent the link to the Wikipedia page to Risse with "WTF?"

DoubleThink: Oh yeah. You're real busy. Pen, you have to take your classes more seriously.

+g00d: And so the apprentice becomes the master.

DoubleThink: You hate it when people quote movies!

+g00d: That's right, I do. What am I become?

DoubleThink: I knew college would ruin you, but I hoped you'd get hooked on sex and drugs.

+g00d: Bah. I already have the internet, which, I have heard, is for pr0n.

"Okay, internet. What else have you got? Thrill me," Penny said.

E.T.'s home planet was called Brodo Asogi—the Green Planet—and it was somehow also in the *Star Wars* universe. These things sure got incestuous, didn't they? But that was *Star Wars*, not *Stargate*. Ugh. This had been more Evan's thing. If it had the word "star" in its title, he liked it. How did he keep it all straight?

This was frustrating, but it was nice remembering him without feeling bad about it. It was almost like Evan was alive again, playing along with her. She imagined his voice prompting her: *If E.T. were going to dial home, what would he dial?*

No, no, no. She was *not* going to figure out the coordinates for Brodo Asogi and then match them to the Stargate glyphs fans had posted online just so she could find the numeric spatial coordinates—and wherever they might lead her. That couldn't possibly be what she was supposed to do. Forget it. She was out. She had real homework to do.

28-26-5-36-11-29 (GEEK COORDINATES FOR "TERRA") — ROSEBURG, OR

PENNY STARED AT THE COORDINATES matching the glyphs she had found for E.T.'s fucking home planet: 31-13-9-9-23-64.

The door to her room opened, and she jumped. Risse came into her room brushing her teeth and looking bright and cheerful, though she couldn't have gotten much more sleep than Penny.

Of course, any amount was better than zero.

"Did you even go to bed?" Risse asked around a mouthful of toothpaste.

"I think I passed out for ten minutes at my keyboard." Comically, she had woken to find her screen filled with the letter "Z."

"That doesn't count." Risse's hair wasn't in a braid today. Had it been yesterday? The day before?

When had her little sister started styling her hair like an adult, and dressing—

"Is that my tank top?" Penny asked. "And my skirt?"

"I din dink ood mine." Foamy toothpaste dribbled from the right corner of her mouth. *I didn't think you'd mind.*

One of the reasons Penny had decided to stay in Roseburg for college and live at home was to be close to Risse, to watch out for her. But even so, she realized she was still missing out on so much of what was going on in Risse's life.

"I don't mind. What time is it?" Penny asked. Golden morning sunlight was filtering through the wooden blinds of the window. "What *day* is it, for that matter?"

Risse held up a finger and then left the room. She came back a moment later without her toothbrush.

"It's Wednesday, after seven. I have to go to school," Risse said.

"I have to go too, to . . ." Penny pushed up her computer glasses and squinted at the screen. "I'm not going to another planet."

"Huh?"

These coordinates didn't match any latitude and longitude she knew on Earth, at least not anything she could get to.

"Oh, how about I try calling?" Penny said.

"Are you talking to me or talking to yourself?" Risse folded her arms. "Because you aren't making any sense."

Penny had been working on her own since the whole Panjea thing, but the truth was she'd always been better in a team, with her sister, then with Max. She needed someone to bounce her ideas off, someone who could do the same with her. Other people didn't necessarily come up with better ideas, but they helped make the ideas better.

"Sorry. Look at this." Penny retyped the numbers on her screen to resemble a phone number: 311-399-2364.

"Whose number is that?" Risse asked.

"Let's find out." Penny Googled it.

Risse leaned over her shoulder, her breath minty fresh. Penny suddenly felt self-conscious about her own breath and covered her mouth.

Risse pointed at the top result. "It's from that classic hacker movie, *WarGames*. I should really get around to watching it."

Google said it was the number of the supercomputer, Joshua, from the film, which was located at NORAD in the Cheyenne Mountain Complex. A little more digging revealed that this was the same address for Stargate Command. *Fancy that*. It couldn't be a working number, but—

Penny looked at Risse. Risse opened Penny's desk drawer, pulled out one of the burner phones there, and then handed it to Penny. Penny dialed. The number rang. It rang a second time.

The house's landline rang downstairs in the kitchen.

Risse's eyes widened.

"It's just a coincidence," Penny said. Never mind that the house phone hardly ever rang, because everyone used their own cell phones. It was just for emergencies.

The ringing stopped downstairs and on Penny's phone.

"Hello?" A woman's voice. One Penny knew well.

"Mama?" she said.

"Penelope, I thought you were upstairs." Her mother sounded confused, but she wasn't as confused as Penny was.

"I am. I, uh, accidentally dialed the house when I was messing with my phone."

"Oh, okay. I'm heading to work. I didn't see your sister leave yet."

"She's right here, Mama," Penny said.

"Well, don't let her miss her bus."

"Don't worry. I'll drive her," Penny said.

"Thank you. Oh, I'll be home late again. Picking up a second shift."

"Okay."

"See you later. I love you."

"I love you too." Penny disconnected the call. Shaken, she needed a moment to stop herself from freaking out.

WHAT THE FUCK?

Penny stared at the cell phone. Someone was messing with her, and dragging her family into it.

"How did you? Why? What the what?" Risse stammered.

"I don't know!"

"What are you involved in?" Risse asked. "I think it's time you shared, don't you?"

"It's a game. It's only supposed to be a game."

Penny had to assume that this, too, was a pointed message from the person or persons behind Gyaraga 1981. We know who you are. We know where you are. And what? Were they threatening to expose Penny as a hacker? Or something worse?

Did they know about Risse being DoubleThink?

Any number of people—people with serious resources—could want revenge on Penny, but there were easier, less convoluted ways both to incriminate her and intimidate her. They just had to pick up the phone and place a tip to the FBI, and the Polonsky sisters' lives would become enormously complicated. More complicated than they already were.

Hold on. Penny had found Gyaraga 1981 on her own. She had sought it out, not the other way around. How would anyone else even have known she was playing, or how to manipulate the clues if she did? Unless whoever was running the game had figured out who Penny was and taken a particular interest in her.

Whatever this was, it was definitely not a game anymore. Maybe it never had been. Gyaraga 1981 had abruptly become very personal, and now Penny had even more motivation to get to the bottom of it.

Calm down, P-squared, Penny thought to herself. She stood and started pacing the room, a bad habit she'd picked up from Max—that was how he put puzzles like this together. She looked at her fingernails, but her own nervous habit was to bite her fingernails, and the paint had chipped away so now they read: "DO PANIC."

Great. That's helpful.

She looked at Risse. "I have to catch you up on some things, but if I tell you now, you'll be late for school."

"If you drive me, we have another half an hour. More like forty minutes, the way you drive. And we can talk more on the way." Risse sat down on Penny's bed.

Penny explained how she'd followed the bread crumbs so far. Risse nodded along. Just as Penny had thought, Risse had heard of Gyaraga 1981 before but had never been curious enough to dig deeper. There was plenty enough to occupy her with problems that mattered.

"Aside from the fascinating question of how they did this, right now I'm more interested in *why*," Penny concluded.

She had been playing along, maybe not as fast as they'd liked. She'd figured it out, hadn't she? But it seemed like they were punishing her and ending the game early. Maybe they wanted her to back off.

Or maybe this wasn't a dead end. She could have missed something. And the message could be that the stakes were higher than she'd thought.

Continue? Y/N

Penny turned back to her computer. The E.T. game screen was still there, but when she refreshed it, a new countdown appeared at the bottom. It stayed frozen for a moment while the page loaded: 261321. When she clicked on the mouse impatiently, the number started decreasing.

The format was strange but it seemed to be counting down by seconds, which made the whole number in seconds. She popped open her calculator app and did the math: 261,321 divided by 60 was 4,355.35 minutes, which was . . . 72.59 hours.

"This is about a three-day timer," Penny said.

This countdown felt much more ominous. Even the extra-terrestrial seemed sinister now.

"Phone home." Penny shuddered. She had actually done that. She needed more. Another website, a new set of coordinates, *something*.

"Let's get you to school. We can pick this up in the car," Penny said.

GOING NOWHERE FAST — ROSEBURG, OR

SEPT. 19, 07:31 A.M.

"THINKING ABOUT E.T. ALWAYS MAKES me crave Reese's Pieces," Risse muttered. She had loaded the countdown page onto Penny's burner phone while Penny drove. "Maybe the next clue has something to do with Atari?" She tapped at the screen. "Their headquarters is at 475 Park Avenue South in New York. But they aren't even making games anymore."

"What about in 1983, when that game was made?" Penny asked.

That took only a little longer to find out. "417 Fifth Avenue," Risse said.

"Can you get a street—"

"Already on it." Risse studied the screen, pulling and pushing around the images on her map with her fingertips. "Okay, there's a jewelry store there now, and a— Oh. Huh."

"What?" Penny risked a glance at her sister.

"There's one of those new Panjea bookstores there."

Penny had thought it was weird when the social media network began opening brick-and-mortar stores, but it must have been working for them, because physical stores were popping up all over the place. Max suggested that Panjea was trying to diversify in the wake of the Silence of Six scandal that they had caused, but Penny thought that was giving themselves too much credit. Gwendolyn Dixon just liked real books, and Panjea had more money than she knew what to do with.

"Panjea! That's it. I'm out," Penny said.

"Really?" Risse said.

Penny sighed. "No, but this doesn't feel good. Anything else?" Penny asked.

"Yeah. The address also lists a 'Panjea Locker' inside the store. Some service they offer for holding mail in a locker for pickup. Oh, and this is cute: They name their locker systems. This one is called Joshua!"

"That's it!" Penny said.

"What's it?" Risse asked.

"Joshua. The computer in *WarGames*. The phone number!" She slapped her forehead. "And E.T. Duh! That stands for Eastern time zone." The car drifted to the left before she pulled it back into her lane.

"Penny! Careful," Risse said.

"Sorry," Penny said. "But there's gotta be something in that locker! Do we have someone we can trust in DP who lives in or near NYC? We could tell them—"

"You're not going yourself?"

"I'm not walking into a Panjea store, not when someone clearly knows who I am. They aren't our biggest fans. Can't imagine why."

"But don't you want to see how this ends?"

"It can end with me going back to my normal life until whomever we send gives us the next clue."

"*What* normal life?"

"Valid point."

"There's more where that came from. You said it yourself. These guys know who we are. Maybe it's too late to stop playing along," Risse said. "They may not let you leave it alone."

"But I can't skip out on any more school right now. And this is barely enough to go on."

"Now you're just making excuses. We've done way more with less. And please don't pretend that you actually want to be in class instead of tracking this down. "

Penny flinched. Her sister knew her better than she'd like to admit.

"What am I supposed to do at a random bookstore in New York in three days?" Penny protested.

"It clearly isn't a *random* store. You can figure it out on the way. Or on the spur of the moment. You're good at that. And I know you can afford a flight to New York."

"I don't know . . . ," Penny said.

"Pen, you should go. You need to—" Risse stopped.

"I need to what?" Penny asked.

"Do something other than babysit me."

"Oh." Penny leaned back in the driver's seat and stared straight ahead, but she was giving only part of her attention to the road.

They were quiet until they arrived at Roseburg High School. Penny's breath caught as she looked at the building she'd spent the last four years in. In the same moment, it felt comfortable and natural to be back there, and it reminded her of how she'd wanted to get as far as possible from her hometown after graduation. How had she forgotten that? Risse was right.

Penny hadn't been excited about anything in a long time. She'd felt such a rush when they figured out where the next part of the game led—she'd felt like herself again. And that brief moment of joy had died as soon as she rejected the idea of leaving home to pursue it. She needed to move on. The only thing worse than failing to be a good hacker, or sister, or girlfriend was failing to be Penny Polonsky. P-squared.

Evan had always known who she was, before she did. She was going to New York, not only to find the next piece of the puzzle, but to find the person she was meant to be.

"On the other hand, I've always wanted to visit the Big Apple," Penny said. She would look at it as a spontaneous vacation, and if she happened to be in the neighborhood of this Panjea store, she may as well stop in. Right. "Okay, I'll go. Wanna come with?"

"That'd be fun. But you know—my life's here and I can't

keep putting it on hold for this stuff," Risse said.

"Right. Your big date?" Penny hated to miss it. But something told her Risse and her beau wouldn't mind if she was out of their hair.

Babysitting? That's what you think, Risse?

Risse smiled. "You know Mama would never let me go to New York, anyway. Especially not on a school night."

Penny did know. But that was no longer a problem for her, and it was time she acted like it.

NEW YORK CITY

PENNY COULDN'T REMEMBER THE LAST time she'd been in a bookstore. She tended to order books online or through her library, when she had time to read, and most of her college textbooks were electronic anyway. She was impressed that even on a weekday morning the store was full of people browsing, reading, taking selfies, just kind of hanging out like they didn't have anywhere else to be.

It was a cliché, but after two days in the city, Penny loved New York. No, she ♥ NY.

Penny had been worried it would be overwhelming, but when you were surrounded by 8.5 million other people, you could be as anonymous as you wanted. It was a hacker's paradise—a coffee shop practically on every corner, free public Wi-Fi everywhere, even in the subways.

Being here cut down on some of the jealousy she felt about Max's European adventure; he'd often talked about going to New York, but she had made it first. He didn't even know she was here! She took lots of pictures, thinking to share them with him later.

As she walked through Panjea Books, she looked for anyone who appeared to be looking for her. Of course she had tried to make it hard for anyone to recognize her as Penny Polonsky. Today she was dressed as her other persona Emmie Steed, who happened to fit right in with current New York fashion: Warby Parker glasses; red, military-style jacket; ivory chiffon blouse; black pencil skirt. High heels would have been more "authentic," but she couldn't give up the sensible flats, in case she needed to run.

She looked just like most of the other young professional women hurrying about on their morning commute to their jobs. Penny felt like she was cosplaying as an adult.

She noticed a tall white guy in a blazer and a *Goonies* T-shirt who always seemed to be in her line of sight. She wandered aimlessly from the self-help aisle to the media criticism section to confirm that he was following her. If he was tailing her, he was crap at it. Every time she glanced his way, he looked down or snatched a book from a shelf and pretended to look at it.

This hipster isn't following me, she realized. *I mean, he is, but . . . I think he's checking me out?* That didn't make her feel much better, but she made sure she knew where *he* was at all times.

She pretended to browse and adjusted her sunglasses. One big problem with a city like New York: cameras. Everywhere. Surveillance cameras, ATMs, tourists with cell phones.

Right at the front of the store was a wall of green and white lockers. She wandered closer. The rectangular compartments came in three sizes: small, medium, and large, numbered from 1 to 100. In the center was a touch screen and a small metal keypad.

She had to wait behind two other customers: a short redhead and a tall, thin black woman with freaking fairy wings strapped to her back and a red barbed tail. Halloween was a month away, but still . . . only in New York! Penny watched her pick up her package.

It looked simple enough. Punch in a six-digit code and one of the locker doors popped open. Tinkerhell didn't even seem to know which door it would be.

Penny stepped up to the screen. Of course there was a camera right over it. But hey, she wasn't doing anything illegal, as far as she knew.

The screen displayed:

Hi, my name is Joshua
Touch screen to start

"Hello, Joshua. Shall we play a game?" Penny asked.

Now all she needed was to log in to the terminal with her Panjea username and password—fat chance—or enter a unique six-digit code. Which she didn't have. But like Risse had said, she was actually damn good at figuring this stuff out—even on her own—and she already had one guess.

The latest countdown had started at a specific, six-digit number. She didn't have a photographic memory like Max, but she was pretty sure it had been 261312. She typed it in on the virtual keyboard.

Validating Pickup Code.

A red bar appeared onscreen, and the message changed.

Pickup Code Rejected.

Damn!

She tried again. 261321.

Validating...

Green!

Pickup Code Accepted.

"Yes!" Penny said.

Now which locker was her package in?

A tone sounded—and *all* the lockers popped opened at once.

"What?" Penny said. "Oh, shit."

The tone was still playing, people were starting to notice. The machine was broken, or . . .

The screen changed to show Penny's surprised face, captured by the locker's camera. Blocky white letters appeared over it:

YOU ARE BEEN PIXELH8TED

"No way." Penny stared at the screen. That was another

blast from the past, but the pieces were starting to fit together.

She still had to get the package and get out of here, and that countdown was almost up. Assuming it wasn't all some elaborate setup, this was probably another test. So there were one hundred lockers; which one had the package for her?

She grinned. There was only one choice. Every geek knew what the answer to life, the universe, and everything was, according to *The Hitchhiker's Guide to the Galaxy*: 42.

She looked in locker number 42, one of the large ones. Pulled out the box. Unmarked brown cardboard, sealed with duct tape. Not sketchy at all, nope. It was heavy and had a plain white label on it that read "C.Q." This clearly had not gone through the postal system, unless they had really lowered their standards.

She peeked in the back of the locker to make sure she hadn't missed anything, then slammed the door shut. The tone stopped, the screen cleared. Now it displayed a jumbled mess of pixels and the word "ERROR."

The word sent a chill down her back. *I hope this all isn't a big mistake*, she thought.

STARBUCKS, THE CITY THAT NEVER SLEEPS (BECAUSE CAFFEINE)

SEPT. 22, 11:09 A.M.

PENNY BEAT A HASTY RETREAT, taking advantage of the confusion as people gathered around the broken Panjea locker. A couple of people pointed at her, and a security guard followed her out of the store and halfway down the block. But another thing New York was good for: large crowds, easy to lose people in.

Penny settled in the closest Starbucks; she had her choice of three in a two-block radius. She ordered the largest coffee they had and sat in a dark corner, near a shabbily dressed man sleeping in a green armchair. Everyone else was keeping their distance, which suited her just fine.

So now she knew at least one of the puppet masters behind this game. "You are been Pixelh8ted" was the calling card of a legendary hacker with the handle H8Bit. He was actually one of the founding members of Dramatis Personai who had been active in the old days of . . .

Well, now all those dated movie references made sense. In fact, rumor had it that H8Bit had been a consultant on *War-Games* and a contributor to one of the first ARG-like experiences on the early internet, *Ong's Hat*. He also had been a hacktivist before the term had come onto the scene, using his considerable powers for good—but he'd disappeared long before Penny took up the cause herself.

If this was really H8Bit, there had to be more going on here. And he wanted the person who opened that locker to know he was involved. Why?

On the other hand, this might not be the original H8Bit. People took over old, abandoned handles sometimes—case in point, the way Risse had assumed full ownership of DoubleThink. There were copycat hackers, trying to steal other people's glory.

People also tried to hijack ARGs; it was possible that Penny had strayed off the path into some alternate-reality game, or the puppet master had lost control of his or her own narrative.

And it had delivered to her a mysterious box.

Now that the moment had arrived, it felt strange to not be sharing this with anyone. She looked around the coffee shop. So many people, living so close together in this city, but they were all strangers to one another—as if the only way to maintain a semblance of privacy was to keep people at a distance emotionally. She didn't know anyone in New York. For a moment, she fantasized about what it would be like to live here one day. Would she have roommates? A best friend to go to parties with and talk about boys?

Penny snorted.

She dialed Risse, but she hung up before the call connected. Her sister was on her way to school right now, living her life. Apparently her date with Emerson over the weekend had gone well enough to merit him a second.

Penny tapped the table with the edge of her phone. It was only five p.m. in Paris right now. She logged in to their usual video chat, but of course Max wasn't online. She sent him a text message anyway. Then she switched to her camera and started recording live video to an unpublished link. It would be sent to Risse and Max automatically in three hours if Penny didn't deactivate forwarding first.

"Okay, so I guess I'm recording my first unboxing video ever," she murmured just loud enough for the mic to pick up her voice. "And yes, this feels pretty stupid, but I don't know what I'm going to find inside this thing."

She peeled the tape off and gingerly opened the box to reveal a black, nylon duffel bag.

"A bag." She lifted it out carefully and turned it over with her free hand. She ran the camera over the white logo printed along it: a lopsided "V." The right side of the letter was crossed with an arrow pointing forward, forming a "T."

"Verbunden Telekom swag? That has to be intentional. It's heavy too. What's in here? Bricks?"

Penny unzipped the bag very slowly. "Please don't be someone's head," she muttered. "Please don't be a head." She pulled
out its contents one by one. She laid them out on the table, making sure the camera picked it all up:

A crowbar. A foldable shovel. A serious-looking pair of
cable cutters. A tactical flashlight, batteries included. A burner
cell phone, the kind that flipped open.

"This stuff can't be for anything good," she said.

She swept everything but the cell phone back into the bag
and put it down at her feet. The phone's notification light was
blinking. She pressed a button, and the screen showed an enve-
lope icon. A text message.

She opened the phone and opened the message:

N 38°54'12.479", W 77°2"34.431".

"That's surprisingly straightforward," she said.

The man in the chair near her opened his eyes and stared
at her.

"Sorry," she said. "Uh, go back to sleep?"

They were latitude and longitude coordinates. *Was this
leading her to some kind of geocache?* she wondered. She stopped
recording and confirmed the video had gotten everything,
including the message with her next destination.

Then typed the numbers into the GPS on her phone to
find out what that was. She got an address: 1828 L St NW #550,
Washington, D.C. Her map showed it as a nondescript structure
on the eastern shore of the Potomac River.

She poked around some more. This building was an old

telegraph office owned by Communications Ltd.

"Oh, that's interesting," she blurted out. The site was also listed on a map of the internet as a collocation data center, one of the many hubs that handled internet traffic around the world. There are maps for that sort of thing, because data nerds loved making maps and charts and infographics. Communications Ltd. was a major connection between the eastern United States and Europe, hooking right into the cables on the seabed of the Atlantic Ocean.

The man in the chair blinked.

"Two months ago, Communications Ltd. was purchased by Verbunden Telekom AG for an undisclosed, but 'significant' sum," Penny told him.

He got up and shuffled away to another seat in the opposite corner.

"Super. I'm the crazy one here." She sighed. "Well, you *are* talking to yourself." Not like there was anyone else to talk to.

She gathered she was supposed to go to this data center. And do what? She doubted she could show up and knock on the door.

Penny went back through the different sites she had followed, but they were gone, taking their clues with them. H8Bit, or whomever was behind Gyaraga 1981, had already cleaned up after themselves.

"Screw it," Penny said. She Googled "Gyaraga 1981" and looked for recent hits. She found a discussion about the game over at reddit.com/r/ARG/. Up until now, she had avoided checking in to see how far others had gotten with the game; other players tended to share information and theories, and that felt sort of like cheating to Penny.

So she was astonished when it appeared that everyone else was playing a different game from her, following different clues. That first website with the countdown had apparently displayed a new link when the time ran out, which had taken players on a merry chase across the interwebs.

At this stage of the game, the other names on the "leader board" had coordinates too, but not for anything in D.C. Local members had been dispatched to a handful of locations across the country, where they had collected black duffel bags— unmarked—filled with . . . puzzle pieces. Hundreds of them. It was clear they all belonged to one large puzzle.

The Gyaragans, as players called themselves, were in the process of painstakingly scanning in each piece and assembling the puzzle digitally. Penny shook her head. Whatever they were doing had nothing to do with the real world. And it was increasingly clear to Penny that whatever puzzle she was attempting to solve had everything to do with real life. The question was, what?

She picked up her almost empty coffee cup and swirled around the remaining liquid, contemplating a refill. Then she nearly dropped it when she saw what was written on the side. Instead of her name—the fake name she had given, "Susan"—the barista, or someone, had written 9/24 24:09 with a black Sharpie.

"What?" Penny jumped up and frantically looked around

the Starbucks. She caught sight of a girl heading for the door quickly. She was about Risse's age, with short red hair, a black tank top that said "Change Your Password," and beige cargo pants. Just before she stepped out the door, she looked over her shoulder and locked eyes with Penny for a split second. Then she was gone.

Penny grabbed her stuff and bolted out onto the street, but the girl was nothing but a memory. In fact, Penny remembered her from before the bookstore; she was one of the people using the Panjea locker to pick up packages. Or perhaps she had been there to drop one off and prime the system for Penny.

Was she H8Bit? She was way, way too young, but she could be working with him, or another hacker who had taken up the mantle.

Penny went back inside the Starbucks and questioned the baristas behind the counter. They all remembered the girl. No, she didn't work there. She'd been hanging out by the pickup station, but they didn't remember her picking up a drink.

As a master manipulator of computer systems, Penny hated being manipulated herself. She thought she'd been playing a game. But H8Bit had been playing her, and threatening her family, or at the very least her anonymity. After dragging her across the country to New York, he now expected her to take another trip to D.C., and judging from the contents of the duffel bag, do some very dirty work.

But from what she could tell, he had also singled her out for this path. He had chosen her from among all the other players—and that was the closest she'd come in a while to getting some recognition of what she was capable of. She hadn't had to hold back, pretend she wasn't up to the task. She hadn't asked for help, not really. And no one else was going to take credit for how far she'd come already.

So she would see this through. She was going to D.C. to win this and find out what happened next. Or she would tell H8Bit to go screw himself. She'd figure it out on the way.

L STREET, WASHINGTON, D.C.

SEPT. 24, 12:01 A.M.

PENNY YAWNED, BELATEDLY COVERING HER mouth even though she was sitting alone behind the wheel of her "borrowed" car. It was a good thing she was a night owl and she was still on West Coast time.

She had already scouted out the building earlier in the day, but there wasn't much out here, which made it extra creepy. Especially late at night.

Penny was hanging out waiting for 12:09 a.m. and whatever was going to happen. Right on time, she heard footsteps echoing down the empty street. In her rearview mirror, she saw a dark shape pass under the orange glow of a streetlight—a man dressed in a black puffy coat and jeans, a duffel bag like hers slung over his shoulder. From his height, the way he walked, his dark hair, he reminded her of Max.

Max hadn't replied to her text message for almost a full day. He'd apologized, said his phone had run out of power while he was making a day trip to some little French village. Yes, that could be true, but Penny had lost the urge to tell him about the wild Google chase that had led her to D.C., so she hadn't responded to his increasingly urgent messages. She wasn't even sure why. It wasn't just that she wanted the satisfaction of doing this by herself. Part of her worried that he was trying to distance himself not only from hacking, but from her. It turned out that she needed a little distance herself.

Penny tensed as not-Max approached her side of the car. She started the engine, stepped on the brake, and put the car into drive. She was ready to put the pedal to the metal if he gave her the slightest provocation. She double-checked that the doors were locked. The man leaned over and tapped on the glass.

Is there a code phrase? Penny thought frantically as she lowered the window. She said the first thing that came to mind, at the same time he did:

"Are you H8Bit?"

They stared at each other and laughed.

Up close, he looked nothing like Max, and not just because he was Asian. He was much thinner, almost scrawny, his true size all hidden by the puffy coat. He was pale too, almost vampiric in the harsh light of the streetlamps, with dark smudges under his bloodshot eyes. He had a scraggly mustache and stubble on his chin that looked like it would never become a full beard. And his right ear was pierced; a tiny red-and-white ball dangled from it.

"What am I thinking? You couldn't be H8Bit," he said.

Penny clenched her jaw. "Because I'm a woman?"

"No, you're too young, by at least thirty years."

"He's way retro, isn't he? You're about my age too, huh?"

"Twenty-five?" he asked.

"Same," Penny lied. "Should I get out, or do you want to come in?"

"I'll sit and get warm, if that's okay. I walked from downtown, and it's cold tonight. Plus I have no idea what we're waiting for."

He came around to the passenger side and sat down, balancing his duffel bag on his knees. He reached over to shake her hand.

"I'm Missing Number," he said.

She snorted. "That's appropriate." She furrowed her brow. "Hold on, you mean 'MissingNO'?" She pronounced the handle the way she always had: "missing no."

He nodded excitedly, his earring bobbing about. "Yeah! You've heard of me?"

"Your video game hacks are incredible," she said. "I'm +g00d."

He screwed up his face. "I don't know that one."

"It's a new handle. I've been around for a while, but I'm sort of reinventing myself," Penny said.

"You could tell me, but you'd have to kill me?" MissingNO smiled.

"I'd never joke about that," she said seriously.

His smile faded.

"So what—" Penny was cut off by a series of tones that she immediately recognized: Dash-dot-dash-dot dash-dash-dot-dash dash-dot-dot dot.

She and MissingNO pulled out their phones.

"Mine," MissingNO said. "A 311 number."

Penny frowned, slightly disappointed H8Bit hadn't chosen to call her.

"I'll put it on speakerphone," MissingNO said.

"Good morning, angels!" said a jovial voice.

"Nope," Penny said. "It's the middle of the night. What are we doing here?"

"Direct. I like that," the man said.

"Are we speaking with H8Bit?" MissingNO asked.

"Yes, but you can call me Nick. My name is Nicholas Phillips."

Penny's jaw dropped. *Why'd he tell us that?*

"I'm sure you're asking yourself why I told you my name. I know I haven't earned your trust yet, but you wouldn't be here if I didn't believe we could trust you," H8Bit said. Nick. "Besides, we already know both of you, so it only seems fair."

"'We'?" she asked. *Is Gyaraga 1981 some secret organization after all?*

"Always two steps ahead. If you'll indulge me, your patience will soon be rewarded," Nick said.

Penny and MissingNO looked at each other.

"I'm Tylor Ayukawa," MissingNO said.

Penny chewed her lip. She considered lying, or sticking with her handle, but it wasn't like MissingNO—Tylor—wouldn't figure it out eventually, and it could be useful to show some good faith upfront. Though that didn't come easily for her.

"Penny," she said. "Polonsky."

She took a deep, shaky breath. She slowly relaxed her hands, which had been gripping her knees, and wiped her sweaty palms on her jeans. She actually felt good, like she had wriggled herself free from a burden she'd been carrying on her back.

It only took a moment for Tylor's eyes to widen as he figured out why she looked so familiar, and why she might be trying to reinvent herself. Penny could practically see him reevaluating everything he knew about her involvement with the hacker named 503-ERROR—Max—and Panjea.

He's quick. I can see how he made it this far, she thought. He had to be at least as good as Penny.

"Now that you've both met, your mission, should you choose to accept it, is to proceed to the GPS coordinates I sent you. There you will find a manhole cover. Open said manhole, descend to its inky depths, and cut the fiber-optic cable therein."

"Say that again?" Penny asked.

"Cut the cord! Everyone's doing it these days. Tonight, anyway," Nick said.

"But that would disrupt internet service? Like a lot?" Tylor's voice went high and squeaky.

"I knew you were a smart lad," Nick said.

Penny squinted. "First of all, that's ridiculously criminal behavior. Second of all, why would we do that?"

"And third, why us?" Tylor asked.

Penny rolled her eyes. *Tylor, you're cramping my style.*

"Imagine, if you will, that the, uh, sensitive information that motivated you to come here is sitting on a hard drive somewhere inside that building. If you cut off the ability for said hard drive to convey its data to the people outside, that information is essentially lost."

"But that's not how the internet works," Penny said.

"That's why I asked you to imagine it," Nick said.

Tylor's expression reflected just what Penny was thinking. *This guy is bananas.*

"I thought you wanted us to trust you. This makes me kind of not," Penny said.

"Understandable. However, I am true to my word. If you cut that cable, in the next half hour, I will delete your personal information in its entirety and never divulge your secrets to anyone."

Penny glanced at Tylor, wondering what he was in for. Tylor's eyes shifted away.

"I'll do it," Tylor said.

"Tylor! Let's talk about this," Penny said.

"Don't need to. This isn't the worst thing I've ever done. The disruption will be temporary. They'll have it fixed in a couple of weeks at most."

"Exactly. So why do it at all?" Penny asked.

"Panjea is still in business. People continue to flock to sign up on it," Nick said. "They have *bookstores*, so now they know what everyone's reading. You must have suspected that would be the outcome of your bold actions, so why did you try to stop them, Penny?"

"To . . . make a statement. Because what they were doing was evil and dangerous, and people needed to know about it. Because I hoped that I was wrong and people would pay attention." Penny took a breath.

She'd been feeling bitter that after what she, Max, and Risse had suffered, after what had happened to Evan, that it all had been for nothing. But it hadn't been. She had done what she'd intended—most of it. People were still talking about Panjea. Remembering the people who had died.

People were waking up. At least she hoped they were. But what if Nick was right? What if everything she and her friends had been through wasn't enough to make a difference?

Penny looked out the windshield of the car she had stolen. She thought about the countless sites she'd hacked, the credit cards she had spoofed, the pizzas she had gotten for free. This was different. She was going to get her hands dirty doing this. And she was going to be attacking the very thing she loved, in the most barbaric way possible.

"Just cut the cables? That's it?" Penny asked.

"That's it," Nick said. "I planned for both of you to attempt this, but you can do this on your own, Tylor. As long as it happens in the next thirty minutes."

If she didn't do this, Risse was at risk of being exposed. Penny had no hope of having the normal kind of life her sister could. She didn't want that, but everything Risse had—and her entire future—could be taken away if her identity was revealed to the wrong people. Setting aside the inevitable government crackdown, DoubleThink had made some enemies in Dramatis Personai for turning against fellow hackers, and Risse would become an easy target.

"Okay," Penny said.

THE INTERWEBS, UNDER L STREET, WASHINGTON, D.C.

SEPT. 24, 12:30 A.M.

THE GPS COORDINATES WEREN'T PRECISE. While they searched for the manhole, they compared notes on how they had gotten there. Their paths had diverged early on.

"When I played that music video with Slim's song, I noticed that it was half an hour long. The video looped the music over and over again. I saw a flash and realized there was a number hidden in a single frame every three minutes. I put them together and got an IP address for a website," Tylor said.

"Damn," Penny said. "Why didn't I see that?"

"I wonder what it means, if the way we got here matters," Tylor said.

"You think there are others?"

"I know there are," Tylor said. "I know a couple of other hackers who were in the running, but I don't know if they made it. We heard about another group that tried to figure the puzzle out together, and they were cut off, so we didn't dare risk it."

After five minutes, they finally stumbled across the manhole cover. It was very old, and at the center was the outline of a cog around a bell icon and the letters "C&P. TEL. Co."

"This should be behind a fence," Tylor said. "Why isn't there any security?"

"I don't even see cameras." Penny tsked.

The company was almost asking for something like this to happen.

Tylor turned out to be surprisingly adept at opening manhole covers with his crowbar, hooking it open and sliding it off in three seconds flat. Penny volunteered to go down the hole while he held the light for her.

"Really?" Tylor asked.

"I can handle it." She stripped off her pink parka and then tucked the cable cutters into the waistband of her black jeans. She slid the tactical flashlight into a front pocket.

"I'm sure you can. But, like, why?"

She smiled. "When am I ever going to have another chance to do something outrageous like this? Do you want to do rock-paper-scissors?"

He held up his hands and pushed the air. "All yours. I'll hold the light and keep watch."

It was only as Penny descended into the manhole that she considered this all could be a setup. Maybe this was the final test, and it was down to the two of them. She imagined Tylor sliding the manhole cover back into place over her head, sealing her inside a fetid tomb with cables and rats.

That's it, no more horror movies for you, Penny.

The metal rungs of the ladder were cool and slick, the air slightly warmer and damper than it was outside. Just a few steps down, the cables were already running thick, bundles of old Cat 5 crisscrossing the narrow space and jammed wherever they would fit. It was a mess of yellow, blue, red, green . . . a true rainbow connection.

She kept moving downward, looking straight ahead as she stepped carefully down, rung by rung. When Tylor shifted the bright LED light above, shadows moved around Penny eerily. The tunnel smelled less like a sewer and more like a server room—the distinct odor of rubber and metal and overheated electronics.

Her feet finally hit cement. Her sneakers splashed in a shallow, greenish pool of water.

Someone's gotta find that leak, she thought. Maybe she'd be doing them a favor, forcing them to come back down here to repair the damage and run new cable, inspect the chaos of cabling.

"How's it look?" Tylor called down.

"A whole lotta cables down here," she said. "Should I cut all of them?"

"I think just the optical fiber," Tylor said. "No telling what else is down there."

"Right." The newest-looking cables were bundles wrapped

in a protective black Kevlar sheath, flexible but tough. She pulled out the cable cutters, opened them, and set the blades around the closest bundle.

"Am I really going to do this?" Penny said.

"*We're* gonna do this," Tylor said.

Penny started to squeeze the cable cutters, testing the strength of the tube protecting the precious data cables within it. It was strong.

"This is safe, right?" She felt like she should have gloves. "Maybe I should have gloves."

A pair of mittens dropped onto her head.

"Thanks."

Penny pulled the gloves on. She gripped the handles even tighter. She gritted her teeth.

I can't.

But she did. She squeezed with all her might. She had to twist the cable cutters around a bit to help them cut through the thick plastic tube, grunting with the exertion. Yet once she got past it, the blades snipped through easily. Penny flinched. It felt like she had cut off one of her own arms.

She stared at the broken cable, the exposed fiber cables inside.

"Holy shit," she said. "What did I just do?"

She couldn't believe she'd actually vandalized private property and directly hurt the internet, a resource that she firmly believed belonged to everyone. She didn't even know who she was working for, who could have benefited from her actions.

Her hands were shaking, and her heart was pounding. It took her a moment to realize that Tylor was shouting down to her in a hoarse whisper.

"I saw . . . I think I saw a flashlight. Someone's walking around the building. We should go!"

Penny nodded. She was so done here.

SPEEDING EAST ON ROUTE 50, LEAVING D.C.

SEPT. 24, 12:42 A.M.

BACK IN THE CAR, TYLOR drove while Penny sat in the passenger seat, practically vibrating with the adrenaline rush. The first sign of their handiwork was their inability to get a signal on their cell phones.

"Not good," Penny said. "We did some real damage back there."

"You think?" Tylor laughed. He sounded giddy. Almost manic.

Penny sort of got it. She was both horrified at what she had done and amazed. Her actions had an immediate, significant impact on other people. She felt powerful in a way she hadn't in a long time. Because of something she did, thousands of people couldn't Netflix and chill tonight, or look up stuff on Wikipedia, or update their Panjea page.

Take that, Panjea!

Yes, when people started waking up in a few hours, this would disrupt their routines. They couldn't read the morning news, check for weather updates, read their important emails. The workday would be disrupted. But all those things were inconveniences. Maybe when it all came back, they wouldn't take it for granted anymore. Penny knew how awesome and powerful the internet was—she lived on it every day. But most people didn't even think about one of the most important tools in their lives. Today, that would change.

Penny's cell phone buzzed. She answered it on speakerphone.

"Superb work," Nick said.

"What happened?" Penny asked.

"Washington D.C. is effectively off the grid."

"That's what I don't get. We couldn't have done that with just those cables," Tylor said.

"There were five other teams cutting cables at separate locations," Nick said.

Penny started to feel queasy.

"What about our deal?" she asked.

"As I said, that information will never get out now. I wouldn't have thrown you or your families under the bus anyway, but now you can rest easy knowing that the information has been erased permanently."

"Okay," she said. "Thanks. But what's this really all about? What we did tonight . . . that isn't sustainable."

"We just kicked the U.S. government off the internet. We cut off large chunks of the Eastern Seaboard and other parts of the country from communicating overseas. Many others are experiencing a dramatic slowdown in service."

"The city will be back to business as usual in a week or so," Penny said.

"I'm counting on it. We'll be studying exactly how they recover from this," Nick said.

"This was a test," Penny said.

"Yes. We weren't just testing your potential as new recruits. It was also a proof of concept for a much bigger initiative, which will make a statement no one can ignore. Tonight was an invitation to both of you to take part."

"Why would we want to keep helping you? You threatened my—people I care about," Penny said.

"We apologize, but we needed you to be motivated and distracted by your personal feelings. The stakes are that high, and then even higher still."

"Who are you working for?" Penny asked.

"That would be telling. But piece it together. Just ask yourself what all these targets have in common. You'll need the internet for that, so you'll do that when you get back home. Once you've figured that out, decide whether you want to get more involved, and then send me an encrypted email using this PGP key fingerprint."

Their cell phones dinged with a new text message:

DCC3 8A16 96DE CB5B 220F BDB7 5E84 BD4F 3A64 A400

"And then what?" Tylor asked.

"Are you up for a little travel?" Nick asked.

That wasn't even a question for Penny. Especially not now. She had always wanted to see more of the world. As a hacker, unless she was doing on-site penetration testing, she could work from anywhere. And businesses would potentially pay her to travel to them. But she had built up her professional identity as Emmie Steed and half-a-dozen other personas, all of which were her, so she couldn't go full-time and on the level without outing herself as a hacker first.

Still, she wasn't ready to give up her power to change the world for the better, and right now that relied on secrecy.

"Depends on where," Penny said.

"Penny, what do you think of Berlin?" Nick said.

Berlin?

"It's supposed to be beautiful this time of year," Penny said.

"You'll have to let me know," Nick said.

"What about me?" Tylor asked.

"London."

"Sweet."

Penny narrowed her eyes. "If you're sending me to Berlin, you must be working with—"

"Don't say their name," Nick said.

She stopped short of speaking "Ada Kiesler" aloud. "So I'm guessing our targets are all related to a certain major media company that's been buying up internet real estate lately. So what is this? Vengeance? Getting hackers to do her dirty work?"

"Not vengeance, Penny. Justice. What do you say? Are you in?"

"I need to read the fine print first," she said.

"It's the same as always: This is illegal and potentially dangerous work. And you can't tell anyone about what you're doing. *Anyone*. Including DoubleThink and 503-ERROR."

Well, that confirmed how much he knew about Penny and her connections.

Doing this required her to give up her life as she knew it. No more college. She'd be lying to her mother and Risse and keeping Max in the dark. It also put Penny at a new level of risk she wasn't prepared for: operating in the field on her own, depending on strangers to have her back. Trust didn't come easy to her; even with Evan's glowing endorsement of his best friend, it had taken her a long time to accept Max as a partner, in every sense of the word.

"I'm not sure I'm the right person for this job." Max would be a better choice. Hell, even Risse would be better at whatever this was. She was already looking for ways to put Dramatis Personai to work helping Ada Kiesler.

"I think you're the perfect person for this. Both of you. I hope we can find out together," Nick said.

Penny glanced at Tylor. He was grinning. His mind was made up. She wondered what he was giving up, or running away from.

They had worked well together so far, but it felt like some kind of betrayal to be joining up with another team. Would Max be jealous? Worried about her? He'd headed off on his own without giving her much consideration. But Nick wanted her help, and if she signed up for whatever this was, she'd be choosing him and Tylor.

It was almost like having friends in real life for a change.

As for Risse . . . she didn't need Penny watching over her anymore—holding her back. She was happy at home, dabbling in hacktivism safely, more or less. Finishing school. Going on dates.

ZOMG. How was Risse's second date going?

Penny sighed. That wasn't the life she lived. Penny needed to be out there helping to make that life possible for other people. She had already helped save the world as she knew it. Now she wanted to see what she had been fighting for.

Penny returned Tylor's smile.

"I'm in," she said.

1985

BRAD STEIN SIGHED AS ANOTHER cluster of fast-moving ghosts swarmed his warrior. What kind of fighter couldn't shoot and walk at the same time? It wasn't like chewing gum.

Shoot or Avoid Ghosts popped up on the arcade game's screen.

"You think?" he muttered. He rapidly pressed the Fire button, slick with sweat and pizza grease, as his character grunted and lost health at an alarming rate.

"*Remember, don't shoot food,*" the game said in its smug electronic voice.

"I know!" Brad said. The voice sounded like a caffeinated Speak & Spell, but it was one of the most impressive things about *Gauntlet.*

"*Warrior—shot food!*"

"Shit." Brad mowed down the remaining ghosts and took out the pile of bones spawning them. The game was a technical marvel, and Brad kept getting distracted as he tried to figure out how it was programmed. Not that he could ever do anything like it, considering he had just botched another C++ assignment.

"Warrior needs food—badly!"

"Shut up," Brad said.

Since the game had appeared in a corner at Koronets, home of "jumbo" pizza slices as big as your head, Brad had lost a lot of quarters to the machine—and done a lot less laundry as a result. He reached into his pocket for his last quarter. He hesitated. He furtively sniffed his armpit. *Eh.* He slid the quarter into the slot to buy his suffering warrior more health.

The movie theater ads said it was "the most fun you can have with a quarter," but it was more like "the most fun you can have with a roll of quarters." This game was punishing, even harder than *Ghost n' Goblins*, his previous arcade obsession. He'd at least managed to finish that—only once, but it was enough to nab the top score. Stupid game.

Brad grunted as he encountered a swarm of grunts. He smoothly maneuvered his warrior with the joystick to nab another key, then a potion, and then he aimed his tiny pixelated avatar for the exit. Brad hunched over the cabinet and stared into the depths of the screen, making it most of the way through another level before he was distracted by shouting outside the pizzeria.

He risked a glance over his shoulder to look out the wide front windows. It looked like a parade or something was passing. People marched slowly down the street, shouting and waving signs in the air. Not a parade, a protest.

Brad started to turn back to his game, but first he scanned

the crowd from habit, looking for . . . Holy crap, there she was!

She stood out from the crowd in her bright red peacoat—which was how he had first noticed her early last month.

It had been a windy September day. Her long black hair billowed around her like she was in a music video on MTV. She was reading a tattered paperback as she moved slowly on College Walk toward Amsterdam Avenue, the wind ruffling its pages.

Brad was late for his Lit class, so as their paths began to intersect he faltered and ended up not saying anything to her. But as soon as she and the moment had passed, he regretted it. From then on, he'd been keeping an eye out for her on campus and in the dining hall, but he hadn't seen her again. Until today.

He'd let her get away once, but not again.

He had nearly broken his highest score in *Gauntlet*, but he pulled his hands away from the sticky controls. He leaned down and grabbed his backpack, then hurried out of the pizzeria. The game called after him: *"I've not seen such bravery!"*

He joined the gawkers on the sidewalk watching the stream of people heading uptown in the middle of Broadway, ignoring the cars honking and angry shouts of people trying to get through. The protestors' signs read STUDENTS SAY NO TO APARTHEID, COLUMBIA DIVEST NOW, FREE SOUTH AFRICA.

Oh, Brad thought. These protests had swept the United States last spring. Students at Columbia had taken over the administrative building for a few weeks, chaining the doors and going on hunger strikes. Brad's mother had even tried to convince him to defer admission for a year, fearing for his safety.

He was pretty sure she was more worried about the debt they were going into to put him through school, though she'd never admit it. So when the protests ended in April, she had no reason to keep him home. She calmed down but made him promise to never get involved in "rabble-rousing" like that himself.

He wondered why they were protesting again. He thought the whole matter had been settled.

Brad ran to catch up to the small cluster of protesters. He slipped into their ranks and worked his way up from the back, his eyes on that familiar red coat. They crossed 112th Street against the light, and a taxicab blocked at the intersection blared its horn at them.

"Free South Africa! Divest *now!*" the protesters around Brad chanted. They were all around his age, and he recognized some of the faces from his classes, but he didn't know any of them. They didn't seem the type to hang out at the Barnard Columbia Science Fiction Society. That wasn't the only thing that made him feel out of place.

It wasn't that Brad didn't like people, but he was far more comfortable interacting with them over a modem or ham radio. And while he supported what the people here were trying to do, he didn't think this was the way to go about it.

"Divest now," Brad said softly, and slightly off in his timing.

He should be back in his room, learning how to code the computer game he wanted to make; catching up on reading for class; watching TV with his roommate, Nick. He should be pretty much anywhere but here.

"Free South Africa," Brad said. It came out sounding more like a question. *Free South Africa?*

A black girl beside him turned and grinned. "First time?" she asked.

"Yeah," he said. "Is it obvious?"

She laughed. "I haven't seen you at our meetings before. Thanks for joining us. It's so hard to get people to care these days, you know?"

That made him feel worse.

"Here." She handed him one of her poster-board signs. STUDENTS SAY NO TO APARTHEID it read in Day-Glo-green bubble letters.

"You sure?" he asked.

"You can make it up to me by coming to the next meeting. Wednesday, seven o'clock, 118 FBH." He nodded.

Brad raised the sign high, jabbing it upward as he chanted, "Divest now! Free South Africa!" Somehow it made him feel less silly, more like part of the group.

As the cluster marched toward 116th Street, Brad worked his way toward the front, toward the girl in red. "Free South Africa! Divest now!"

She was shouting louder than everyone, her voice high and clear and beautiful. Like she was singing. Her long hair was tucked into the collar of her coat, and as she chanted—as she *led* the chanting, he realized—she looked around, challenge glinting in her brown eyes, passion flushing her cheeks. Or maybe that was from the cold. She looked at Brad for a moment, and he heard himself raising his voice to match hers.

"Say no to apartheid!" they chorused in perfect harmony.

Her fury and confidence were infectious. Brad stepped up to the head of the line, now proudly carrying his sign and adding his voice to the others. It didn't matter why he had joined them. Brad felt like he belonged right here, right now, beside her.

Then he caught sight of the officers lined up in front of Columbia's main gates. They weren't wearing the white shirts of campus security; these men were in NYPD blue.

"Holy crap," Brad said.

The protesters stopped in front of the gate, and the chanting fell off until only the woman in red remained shouting. Brad tried to join her, but his throat was dry, and he couldn't form the words. He turned around. He just wanted to leave. He saw a few others had the same idea.

"All right, break it up," one of the officers said in a thick Brooklyn accent. "You've had your fun, kids. We've already been down this road."

"This isn't fun, and we aren't *kids*," the girl said. She spat the word like it was a curse. There was a slight tremble in her voice, but her face betrayed no fear. Her face was also exceedingly pretty. She reminded him of Ally Sheedy.

Marry me, Brad thought.

"This is an unlawful gathering, and you're disrupting the public peace," Officer Brooklyn said. "You don't have a permit to march."

"This is a *protest*," the girl said. "We don't need a *permit*."

"Lianna," said a tall white guy on the girl's other side. She ignored him. Brad leaned forward to get a better look at him. Thin black hair in a scraggly ponytail, pimples sprinkling his greasy forehead. Brad felt a pang of jealousy. But at least he knew her name now.

"Let's go," the guy said. "We've made our point."

"We've only just started," Lianna said.

"Go back to your dorms or you will be arrested for disorderly conduct," Officer Brooklyn said.

"That isn't legal. We have the right to gather and express our opinions," Brad said. He was surprised to hear the words come out of his mouth. He wasn't even sure if they were true. Lianna nodded and smiled at him, which felt like getting a real-life potion upgrade.

"You've done both," Officer Brooklyn said. "Now go home."

"You can't stop us from entering campus," Lianna said.

"Try it," Officer Brooklyn said.

Don't try it, Brad thought.

Lianna tried it. She lowered her sign and then leaped forward. Brad grabbed her arm to stop her. She pulled her arm out of his grip, making him stumble forward, and then she spun and decked him. He saw stars and pain exploded as her fist connected with his nose. He yowled and fell backward, dropping his sign.

The next thing Brad knew, strong arms were grabbing for him, holding him down. People were shouting, scattering, struggling.

"You're under arrest," a gruff voice screamed in Brad's face. "You-have-the-right-to-remain-silent-anything-you-say-can-and-will-be-used-against-you." He rattled the familiar phrase off in such a rush, it all sounded like one word.

"Shit," Brad said.

"Noooooo!" Lianna screamed. "Let me go!" She sobbed. Now she sounded like a frightened kid. And just as her voice had lent him confidence before, her desperation made him even more afraid.

We are in so much trouble, Brad thought.

Brad pressed the blood-soaked sleeve of his sweatshirt to his throbbing nose as he squatted on the cold floor in a corner of the jail cell. The cops hadn't even given him a tissue. He was pretty sure his nose wasn't broken, but it was tender and it would not stop bleeding.

Someone settled down next to Brad, but he didn't open his eyes until he heard her voice.

"How's your nose?" Lianna asked.

He squinted his eyes open and winced as his eyes adjusted to the harsh fluorescent light. His headache intensified.

"I'll live," he said. "Until my parents kill me." *Sorry, Mom.*

"Tell me about it," she said. "Are they coming to pick you up?"

He shook his head. Moving made the pain flare brighter.

"They're in California, thank God. They're wiring money, but not until tomorrow. Dad said I can have a 'night in solitary' to think about what I've done."

He knew the extra expense was going to be yet another hardship for his parents, which was a far worse punishment. On the other hand, he wasn't alone; a night with Lianna didn't sound so bad, even in a jail cell.

"Ouch." She leaned a little closer and lowered her voice. "Sorry I punched you. I thought you were a cop."

"It's a good thing I'm not," he said.

Her eyes widened. "That's true."

"I'm sorry I grabbed your arm." *Really sorry*, he thought. He should have run away with the others.

He never should have gotten involved in the first place. This wasn't like him—running into a situation without weighing all the pros and cons. Running after a girl.

Brad had hoped to reinvent himself from the nerdy, friendless kid he'd been in high school. So far, a month into college, he was still nerdy and he had one friend, if he counted his roommate. But he suspected Nick was only nice to him because he also didn't have any other friends.

Brad didn't want to be alone anymore. He didn't want to be boring. Luke didn't become a Jedi by playing it safe. He'd left behind everything he'd known, made some cool new friends, and kissed a princess. Who had ended up being his sister, but that was beside the point. Brad had never kissed a girl before, and he really wanted to kiss the one right in front of him.

"I guess you were trying to help. So thanks," she said.

"You're welcome." He looked around. Six of them had been arrested, but three of them had already been released, either because of their parents or their lawyers—which were basically the same thing: money. Now the only other occupant of the cell was the tall guy who had tried to get Lianna to leave. He sat on the opposite side of the cell, watching the two of them.

Interesting, Brad thought. He wondered if the two of them were together or not. He wondered if the guy had decided to stay in the cell with her on purpose, or if he was also stuck the way Brad was.

"I'm Lianna," she said. "My friends call me Lee."

"Brad. My friends call me KD6A."

Her mouth quirked. "What are you, a robot?"

"Assumption incorrect," he said in his best impression of K-9 from *Doctor Who*. Then in his normal voice, he explained: "That's my ham call sign. Amateur radio."

"A pleasure, KD6A," she said.

He ran through his possible responses.

If you say, "Nice to meet you, if only it were under better circumstances," turn to page 42.

If you say, "Come here often?" turn to page 86.

If you say, "You're so beautiful! Go out with me?" turn to page 91.

But life isn't a Choose Your Own Adventure book, and Lianna had already moved on with the conversation while he was thinking about what to say.

"So you're from Cali? Like, Los Angeles?" she asked.

"No. I mean yes, I'm from California, but not L.A. I grew up in Granville."

"Oh, Granville!"

"You've heard of it?" Brad was shocked.

"No. Actually, it sounds made up."

"It's only a few hours from San Francisco."

"Awesome. I've never been to the West Coast."

"Where are you from?"

"Right here. I've lived in Manhattan my whole life."

"That must have been exciting though. Lots of people wish they lived here." But not him.

Brad found NYC exhausting. The city was dirty and smelly, and New Yorkers were as rude as everyone said they were. The subway was loud and hot and noisy, and there were rats everywhere. *Everywhere.* He didn't know how people lived practically on top of one another every day; he needed more space. He rarely went off campus, never downtown. And after this little adventure, he wasn't sure if he'd ever leave his dorm again.

"I want to see more of the world."

"So why'd you stay here for college? I couldn't wait to leave home. This was the farthest I could get without leaving the country."

She smiled. "I'm going to travel someday. We went on a family trip to Paris last—when I was fifteen. I never wanted to leave."

"Maybe you can do a semester abroad. What year are you?"
She paused. "I'm a senior."

"Oh. Too late, then." He should have known she was older than him. "What's your major?" he asked, to deflect her from finding out he was only a freshman.

"Making the world a better place." She smiled. "You?"

"Computer science." That sounded kind of pathetic compared to her answer, but he wasn't the best at thinking on his feet. Or sitting on his butt in a corner with a bloody nose. This girl was really intense though.

"Ooh, can you change my grades, like Matthew Broderick in that movie?"

"Um. *WarGames*?" That was one of the movies Nick was obsessed with. He had a bootleg Betamax of it, and he practically ran the videotape on a loop. Actually, Nick probably could change Lee's grades for her.

"Maybe," Brad said. "Depends on the class. Which one?"

She bit her lip. "You know, I haven't seen you at our meetings."

How small were these meetings that everyone knew who went to them?

"I saw what you were doing and just thought I'd join in," Brad said.

"You did?" She grinned. "That's awesome!" She leaned back, a smile still on her face. "That's what I was hoping would happen. You just made my night, Brad."

"That's what I was hoping would happen," he echoed.

She gave him a weird look. *Shoot, that went too far. Now she thinks I'm weird*, he thought.

"You're weird," she said.

"Yeah," he said.

"I like weird, Brad. You'll fit right in with the group. I'm sorry this happened your first time out."

"Me too. To be honest, this was kind of impulsive for me. I don't usually go for this stuff."

Lee tilted her head toward him. "You're not usually impulsive?"

"No. Definitely not. But also, I don't really believe in protests."

Brad noticed Lee's friend look at him sharply.

Lee sucked in a breath.

"I mean, I'm not sure about them. Like, what are you trying to accomplish?" Brad asked.

"We just want people to be aware of what's going on, to take notice. Take action."

"Does that work though? I signed a petition last summer to stop them from reopening Three Mile Island, but that didn't stop them. It's back to business as usual."

She scoffed. "Petitions! But you didn't march? You didn't call and write your representatives?"

Brad shrugged.

"Then you didn't do anything. Signing a petition is just a way to make you feel like you've done something."

"So you don't think petitions make a difference? But marching will."

"People noticed, or they wouldn't have called the cops. You noticed and joined us."

"And got arrested," Brad added.

"But you did something. You made something happen. They couldn't ignore us, or our message."

"You don't really believe our protest will convince the university to change anything?"

"Maybe not this protest, maybe not today or this year. But it isn't entirely about that." Lee pushed her bangs away from her eyes and twisted around to face him, folding her legs under her. "We'll make some headlines, right? And so more people will learn about what we're fighting for. Maybe we won't change anyone's mind . . ." She looked away, faltered. "But we're also sending a message."

"To whom?" Brad asked.

"To South Africa. To South Africans in America. We're saying: We don't approve of this. We're trying to change. We're here to help."

He hadn't considered that the act of protest itself could be beneficial. The way Lee described it, even if it failed in its overt purpose, it still had meaning. "You think they know about what's happening over here?" he asked.

"I hope so. But I'm glad you listened. What motivated you to get involved?"

Brad blinked at her. He barely knew anything about apartheid, except that it was bad and it was something happening very far away that had nothing to do with him.

If you say, "Apartheid totally sucks!" turn to page 33.
If you say, "Who doesn't love South Africa?" turn to page 86.
If you say, "I just wanted to meet you," turn to page 99.

Brad cleared his throat. "Well . . . you did. You're very inspiring."

Lee's eyebrows shot up.

Too much? Brad thought.

"That may be the nicest thing anyone has ever said about me," Lee said.

"Monroe!" A cop stepped into the room and walked up to the bars. He pulled out a ring of keys and slowly inspected each one. "Daddy's here to take you home."

"To be continued." Lee sighed. "Time to face the music. Specifically Chopin, Piano Sonata no. 2."

"Huh?" Brad asked.

She hummed a few bars. "Dun dun da-dun. Dun dada dada da-dun." The funeral song.

"Oh. He doesn't approve of your political activism?" A stern-faced man was standing in the doorway, arms folded. He had broad shoulders and a beefy build. He looked like a linebacker.

"I guess we'll find out, since this is the first he's heard of it. I'm not terribly hopeful."

Lee stood and smoothed out her red coat. "If I had to go to prison, I'm glad I shared a cell with you, KD6A. Maybe I'll run into you at our next meeting."

Ask her out ask her out ask her out.

"Yeah, you too. Good luck," Brad said.

On her way out, Lee tossed a wave at the other guy from the protest. "See ya, Maxwell."

"B-bye, Lianna," he said.

And then she walked out. Not long after, Maxwell was released too, and now Brad was in solitary confinement after all.

The day had begun normally enough. He'd woken up late. Flunked a pop quiz. Skipped Art Hum to finish his CS homework. Fallen asleep in math. Had pizza. Played some *Gauntlet*. Then things had gone off the rails. He'd joined the Rebel Alliance and was imprisoned for a greater cause and met a brilliant, bold, beautiful girl. So basically everything he'd ever wanted from life.

Almost everything—but there was a new hope. He hadn't gotten Lee's digits, but at least he knew her full name now. Lianna Monroe.

He could work with that.

Brad pushed down the switch hook of the pay phone to disconnect the call, his twentieth in as many minutes. The line clicked, and the high-pitched dial tone filled his ear.

He glanced again to his right. He was standing on College Walk, facing Amsterdam, in the direction Lianna—Lee—Monroe had been walking the first time he'd seen her.

It was riskier to do this out in the open, but it was also a little more exciting. Even if anyone saw him, few people would know what he was doing. Still, he angled his body into the phone booth to try to hide his movements as he lifted his red box, a Radio Shack tone dialer, to the mouthpiece of the handset tucked between his left ear and shoulder. He pressed a button, and it played a tone into the receiver. Under the dial tone, he heard gentle clicks as the phone interpreted the signals as a quarter being inserted. He dialed a phone number on the keypad, and his call connected. For free.

The phone on the other end rang once, twice, three times.

"Hello?" a gruff male voice answered.

Brad cleared his throat. "Hi, I'm looking for Lee, um, Lianna—"

"Do you know what time it is?"

"Uh . . ." Brad checked his calculator watch. "6:08."

"Wrong. At the sound of the tone, the time is dinner."

"What?"

"*Beep.*"

"Excuse me? Is Lianna there?"

"Like I said, it's dinnertime."

"I just wanted—"

"We're having Stove Top," the man said.

"I'm sorry. Sir."

"You should be."

"Should I call back later?"

"Why would you do that?"

"Is Lianna there?" Brad asked hurriedly. "Lianna Monroe?

Does she live there?"

"You want to speak to Lianna?"

"Yes! But I'll call back later. I'm sorry for interrupting dinner. I love Stove Top too."

The line was quiet. Had the man already hung up? Brad listened more closely, but he heard breathing.

"Sir?" Brad asked.

"Yes." He was still there.

"Yes, I should call back later?"

"Do you have a message for Lianna?"

"Can you tell her Brad called? No, tell her KD6A called."

"What's your number?"

"That's okay. I'll just call back at a better time," Brad said.

"Why?"

"To talk to Lianna?"

"No one here by that name. Good-bye!" *Click.*

"Sheesh," Brad muttered. Did that guy just wait for people to call the wrong number so he could prank them?

He struck out with his next three calls too. One number never answered, so he marked it on the flimsy torn page from the phone book to try again later. The other two people were much nicer to him at least.

Brad lifted the box to the receiver again, and someone tapped him on the shoulder. He jumped and dropped the box. He considered running.

"Did I scare you?"

Brad froze when he heard Lee's voice. Not from the phone

dangling from the booth, but from right behind him. He turned around.

"Fancy meeting you here," she said.

"Not that shocking, since this is our school." But it was a coincidence that she'd found him while he'd been trying to track her down on the phone. Also, it was a little awkward. He surreptitiously folded the phone book page for "Monroe" and slipped it into his pocket.

He worried she'd think it was creepy that he'd gone to such lengths to try to find her. He'd stopped by the Columbia Student Activism Club meeting on Wednesday, but no one else had shown up; perhaps after the mess the apartheid protest had become, they were taking a break. Or they had decided to meet another time or place, and he had no way of knowing.

Brad also hadn't been able to find Lee in the campus directory. Part of him was impressed that she was so hard to track down. It seemed like a smart strategy for an outspoken political activist. He also thought she must be living at home, but if not, he might be able to convince her parents to give him her number or to pass on a message. Either way, he knew she was from New York, so it seemed the best place to start.

Lee crouched and picked up the black box he'd dropped. "What's this, Mr. Robot?"

The excuse Brad had always practiced—"Oh, that? It's nothing. Just a tape recorder."—died on his lips. "It lets me make free phone calls," he said.

Shut up, Brad thought. He realized he was still trying to

impress her, but now he was admitting to breaking the law. But he could trust her, couldn't he? He wanted to trust her, which wasn't the same thing. But at least she had a healthy disdain for the law.

"You don't say?" Lee handed it back to him. He quickly checked it over for damage. "This is a hacker thing?"

"Sure," he said. "Calling around to other computers gets expensive, but there's almost always a work-around, if you know the right stuff." Or the right people.

"Can you show me?" she asked. "Who were you calling?"

"Oh, no one in particular." He fiddled with the stiff metal cord of the phone's receiver. "Sometimes I just dial random numbers to see who I get, like when I'm DX'ing on my ham radio—listening for active radio signals. You can mess with people too, make them think you know them, but I'm not very good at thinking on my feet."

Lee smiled. "Can I try?"

Brad nodded. He lifted the receiver from the hook and held the red box up to the mouthpiece. "So all this does is trick the phone system into thinking money has been deposited so you can dial. Any number in particular?"

"Surprise me."

He pressed the button several times and then dialed a random ten-digit number. He handed the receiver to Lee.

She listened. "It's ringing!" She giggled. Then he heard the ringing stop on the other end of the line, and a tinny voice said "Hello?"

"Yes, hello! How are you?" Lee asked. She had affected an English accent. "Why, it's Elizabeth. Elizabeth Bennet." She rolled her eyes at Brad, as if she couldn't believe whoever it was didn't recognize her. She was really getting into this.

"Oh, no, I'm calling you back. Yes, I'm quite sure. John left a message for me to call at once. At once!" She paused. "Jim, yes, that's right. I don't know what I was thinking. My brother's name is John, that happens to me all the time. Is Jim there?"

Lee frowned. "No, he was quite clear that I should call today, right this very moment. Are you certain he isn't there? I already told you, it's Elizabeth, dear. Lizzie."

Brad covered his mouth to stop himself from laughing out loud. Lee was really good at this.

"No, you tell him not to bother calling me back. We're through, do you hear me? No, you can ask him that. You ask Jim. He'll tell you all about us. Good day." She paused. "I said 'Good day!'" And she hung up the phone.

She burst into laughter and Brad joined her. "Oh, she was so confused!" Lee said, still using her British accent.

"That was awesome!" Brad said. "I think you just got Jim into trouble."

"Well, it's her fault if she doesn't read Jane Austen." She continued using her fake voice.

"How'd you learn to do an accent like that?" Brad asked.

"My mom grew up in England and I always wanted to talk like her."

"Yeah, it's—" *Hot!* "Impressive."

"Thanks. Speaking of impressive . . . so you're good with computers, right?"

"Pretty good."

"Good enough to hack into the school?"

Brad looked around, checking to see if anyone was listening. He nodded toward Broadway and started walking. She followed him.

He lowered his voice. "Look, I might have exaggerated my skills a little. Like, I know someone who could probably help you, but honestly, you seem pretty together. Are your grades really that bad?"

"It's not for me, not really." She paused.

"I'm not sure how sophisticated their system is. It would probably be easier to just break into the office and log in manually."

She tilted her head, considering. "Okay."

"Okay? What's this about?"

"Brad, I've been thinking about what you said before, about signing petitions and protesting and everything."

"What did I say?"

"That it isn't enough."

Brad frowned. "I didn't say that."

"That was the gist of it, and I agree with you. We probably aren't going to change anything. . . . Or it will take too long for it to be meaningful."

Brad stopped at the corner of 114th Street. "About that. So I did some reading, and it turns out that Columbia's trustees already agreed to divest from companies doing business in South Africa."

She scowled. "Yeah, in two years. It should take less than a year. Nine months, tops."

"But you've already done what you set out to do. They listened. They're working on it."

She shook her head. "They say they're working on it. That isn't the same thing."

"What are *you* saying?"

She glanced down the street and groaned. Brad glanced to his right and glimpsed a black sedan cruising slowly toward them. The driver, a white man in a Blues Brothers hat and sunglasses, was pointing a camera at them.

"What the hell?" Brad started toward the car.

"Leave it," Lee said.

"Do you know who that is? Is he following you?"

"He works for my father," she said.

"Who's your father?" Brad asked. "That's seriously creepy."

"Just ignore him."

"Yeah?" Brad shook his head. But he kept walking. "You have some 'splaining to do," he said in his best Ricky Ricardo voice.

Lee grimaced. "That is the worst Ricky Ricardo impression I've ever heard. Better leave the voices to the professionals."

"Seriously, are you in some kind of trouble?"

She flashed him a lopsided smile. "Almost always. Not you though?"

"Nope," Brad said. "I've always been the perfect kid."

"Except for the illegal phone calls. And getting arrested."

"Those are recent developments." Brad laughed, but nervously. Truthfully, he didn't know who he was anymore. Moving from Granville to New York had done more than expand his world—it had shaken it up. Turned everything upside down.

In the past, back home, it had been easy to think only of himself and his family, but New York felt so much more international than California. It was so different from Los Angeles and the Bay Area, it may as well have been on the other side of the world. In a different universe. He felt pressured to act like someone different, just to try to fit in with the richer, smarter, better-looking kids. "Fake it till you make it," as they say.

There was no putting Jeannie back in the bottle. Brad liked it, but it left him feeling a bit adrift, like every possibility was open to him. That kind of choice made him paralyzed. Maybe that would have been the case no matter what college he'd gone to.

But then he wouldn't have met Lee, and he already knew one thing for certain: Whatever his life became, he wanted her in it.

"My father says I'm just acting out, for attention," Lee said. "But I've never been big on authority. And lately I've been questioning it even more."

Brad paused to look in the window of the hardware store. Out of the corner of his eye, he saw the black car drifting slowly up the street, trying to keep pace with them.

"I can't do this," Brad said. "Come on." He grabbed Lee's hand and pulled her into the pizza parlor.

"I thought you weren't the spontaneous type. Did you suddenly get hungry?" she asked. She didn't let go of his hand.

"Sorry. That car following us is just freaking me out. I know these guys. They'll let us sneak out the back."

"There's no sense in me giving him the slip. He does know where I live," Lee said.

"Well, I don't like him taking pictures of me," Brad said. "You wanna go back out there?"

Lee took a deep breath. "Nah. This pizza smells great, and I haven't had lunch."

"The pizza's only okay, but the slices are massive," Brad said. He caught a frown from Tony behind the counter. He mouthed an apology.

"Size isn't everything," Lee said.

Brad blushed. Tony snorted.

"I'm buying." Lee pulled out a ten-dollar bill.

"Oh. I can't let you . . ." He trailed off. He didn't have any money, of course.

"*Daddy's* buying," she said. "He kind of owes us. Plain okay?"

"Yeah. And, um, could you get some quarters?"

"Sure."

Brad went to stand by the *Galaga* cabinet. He hadn't been playing this one much lately, but only because he had already gotten the highest score. There it was, still at the top of the demo screen: 325,150.

Lee returned from the counter and placed a stack of eight quarters on the machine. "This enough?"

"Thanks. I'll only need one."

"Such confidence. Show me what've got, hotshot."

Brad picked up a quarter and slid it into the slot. "Did you want to play too?"

"Oh, no," she said. "If you're that good, I'm happy to watch. Besides, I don't believe in video games."

Brad pressed the Start button. "What do you mean? There are games right in front of you."

"I know they *exist*, dummy. But I don't believe in wasting time on frivolous things. Not judging, just saying. Maybe a little judging."

"Whoa!" Brad nearly crashed into an attacking bug, but he dodged and shot it down on its next sweep. He frowned when a boss Galaga captured his ship with its tractor beam, but he was slipping into the zone. "I'm not wasting time. This is research. I'm going to program games one day."

She muttered something.

"What?" he asked.

"That's even more of a waste of your talents," she said.

"Hmmm." He tried to hide his hurt feelings. Or was that meant to be a compliment? "Have you been talking to my mother?"

Brad easily recaptured his ship and doubled his firepower.

Now it was a simple matter of mowing down the waves of attackers.

"Well, you *are* pretty skilled at this," she admitted. "Too bad you can't make a career out of playing games."

"Yeah."

"Oh, the pizza's ready."

Brad scooped up the extra quarters and followed Lee and their slices to one of the few tables. He heard his ship explode at the abandoned cabinet behind them.

The best thing about this place was the games. He hardly ever came here to eat, but when he did, he always took his slice and cream soda to the counter. The walls were lined with mirrors, and there was nothing like watching yourself stuff your face with the world's largest pizza. It was also a sneaky way to people watch without being obvious about it.

An Asian girl their age walked into the shop as they sat down.

"Hey, Lee," she said. "Hey, Lee's mysterious boy friend. That's two words, not one, unless . . ." She raised a pierced eyebrow.

"Hi, Kim. This is Brad," Lee said. She shot Kim a warning glance.

What's that about? Brad thought.

"Hello, Brad," Kim said. "I wish I could join you, but I have to get back to class. Should I wait for you, Lee?"

"No, I'm going to be a while," Lee said.

Kim walked away, then glanced behind her and winked at Brad.

"Friend of yours?" he asked.

"I wouldn't say she's a *friend*," Lee said. "I know her from school."

"She goes to Columbia too? She looks like she's fourteen."

"I meant I used to go to high school with her." Lee lifted a gooey slice of pizza and folded it expertly in half. She took a big bite and winced. "Ow, ow, ow! Ah burned mah mouth," she said.

"Careful, pizza's hot," Brad said.

She glared at him.

"Sorry, I always do that too. See?" He chomped down on a pizza slice and winced. "Ow!"

She rolled her eyes. "Goof."

"You provide the meal, I provide the entertainment."

"Fair. But you can treat me next time, and for the record, if you ask instead of dragging me into a random establishment, I'll probably say yes."

"Good to know." Burning the roof of his mouth was totally worth it.

They blew on their slices and munched for a little while. After Lee's friend Kim left, she leaned forward and lowered her voice. "So tell me: You'd rather save video game worlds than the one around you?" Lee asked.

"When you put it like that . . ." He swiped the back of a hand across his mouth. "You make me sound like an asshole."

She shrugged.

"Ouch. I don't think we're quite talking the end of civilization here."

"Tell that to the people suffering in South Africa. What do you believe in, then? Three Mile Island, you said?"

"You have a really good memory." He barely remembered what they'd talked about in that cell together, he'd been so nervous.

"Photographic." She mimed holding up a camera and pressing a shutter button. "Click!"

"I bet that comes in handy." He put down his slice of pizza, suddenly losing his appetite. "I think a lot about technology."

She perked up. "In what sense?"

"So . . . Three Mile Island. The thing about that is, I was reading this book about how complex systems are more vulnerable to flaws in organization and management than technological failure. It's by this guy named Perrow, *Normal Accidents: Living with High-Risk Technologies.* You want to talk about the end of the world, let's talk about nuclear proliferation."

"Technology still comes down to just people," Lee said.

"Exactly." Brad nodded. "And they went ahead with it anyway. It's only a matter of time before it all falls apart. Global thermonuclear war." He took a bite of pizza. "My roommate's obsessed with *WarGames*, but he says that instead of looking at it as a warning that hackers can trigger a war, it gives him hope that hackers can help prevent one."

"A scary prospect either way," Lee said.

"So what about you? What got you into activism?"

She picked at the cheese on her pizza. "The Guerilla Girls."

"The who?"

"No, that's a different group." She smirked. "Honestly, Brad. Where have you been? Oh, right, good old Granville."

"Nothing much exciting happens there," he said.

"The Guerilla Girls—that's G-U-E-R-I-L-L-A—are female artists and activists. They stage protests to fight sexism and racism in the art world, while wearing gorilla masks to keep anonymous."

"Seems cowardly," Brad said.

"Seems smart," Lee said. "Weren't you just saying you don't like being photographed? I think they're very brave. They have way more at stake than you do."

"You care about the New York art scene that much?"

"Not at all—aside from theater, because of my parents. My father's a big donor to local theaters, and Mother's an actress. But that kind of discrimination is worth fighting wherever it appears. I want to be part of something like that. One person can do a lot to change the world. Lots of people can do even more. Maybe you don't win every battle, but you're helping to create a movement. The more you do, the more you can overcome other people's natural apathy and inspire them to get involved."

She was the real deal. She wasn't just spouting some lofty ideas; she wasn't trying to impress Brad. She was truly passionate about the fight, and it was working. She was inspiring. He thought he might follow this girl anywhere, no matter how stupid or pointless he thought it might be.

They were both alike: They wanted to be part of something

bigger than themselves and make a difference. Only Lee was actually making it happen, and Brad was still too concerned about the personal consequences to take risks for other people.

"But apartheid. You think Columbia isn't being honest about it?" he asked.

"I know they aren't!" she said.

An older couple at the table next to them looked over.

Lee ducked her head and lowered her voice. "I know they aren't." She took a deep breath. "My father, he's one of the trustees."

"Of *Columbia*? He must be a big deal."

She shrugged. "He thinks so. He's . . . a Wall Street broker at Pierce and Pierce." Her tone suggested this was worse than being a drug dealer.

"Like in *Trading Places*? He buys pork bellies and frozen orange juice?"

She nodded slowly. "He's totally Louis Winthorpe the third. I overheard him tell Mother the university's only going to drop its high-profile investments in South Africa, the ones the public is aware of. Not only that, but several trustees have their own investments there and aren't planning to change."

"That's . . . heavy," Brad said.

She poked at her pizza. "You know, I'm not hungry anymore. Can we walk?"

"Yeah." Brad looked at his own unfinished slice, wondering if he could bring it with him. He decided to leave it behind.

When they went outside, the Blues Brother was nowhere

to be found. Even so, they headed west toward Riverside Park, where cars couldn't follow.

"So that's why you're continuing to protest," Brad prompted.

"Exactly! But it isn't working. It won't work. The public has moved on. Even the CFSA has moved on. And the university doesn't have patience for this kind of thing anymore, not over this."

Brad rubbed his still tender nose. "Obviously."

"But if we can get the word out, find proof that they're lying . . ."

Brad sighed. "I see where you're going."

"The only problem is: I can't be the one to speak up," Lee said.

"Because you'll expose your dad."

"Basically, yeah. He's a good man, honest. But obviously he isn't perfect."

"Who is?"

They fell silent as they waited for some roller skaters to pass before crossing the street to the sprawling park alongside the East River. They made their way down the stone staircase.

Brad didn't know what to do. Even Lee was afraid of getting into trouble with her dad. If Brad got involved and was caught, he wouldn't have a rich trustee of the university to protect him from expulsion or imprisonment. But the information she had shared with him was like an itch he felt like scratching. He had crossed a line, and he couldn't pretend he didn't know what he knew. How could he go on as if everything was okay?

At the foot of the stairs, Brad stopped and sat on one of the steps. Lee sank down next to him.

"Anyway, unless we have proof, other than something you heard, it's just our word against theirs," Brad said slowly.

Lee smiled.

"What?" he asked.

"Nothing. You were saying . . . ?"

"Um. They have lawyers and stuff—"

"Many of them *are* lawyers and stuff."

"Even worse. And I . . ." Brad swallowed. "We could get kicked out of school for this. Or sued. I can't risk that."

Lee nodded. "I get it. It wasn't fair of me to ask. This isn't your fight."

"It isn't yours either," Brad said.

She frowned. "What do you mean?"

"I don't know. But, like, why do you care so much about strangers on the other side of the planet?"

"It doesn't matter who they are, or where they live, Brad. They're strangers, yes, but they're people. Like us. And they're suffering. That's why I care. Why don't you?" Lee stood up.

"I'm sorry," Brad said.

"Me too. I've gotta go. Nice running into you again, Brad."

"Yeah. Listen, I'll, um . . . think about it, okay? How do I get in touch with you? You know, if I have to, um . . ."

Lee stared at Brad for a long moment. "212-555-2368." Then she walked off.

Brad repeated the number to himself as he walked back to

his dorm, jingling the spare quarters in his pocket. As a date, lunch hadn't ended well; he'd thought there was something developing between them, but Lee might be interested more in how he could help her than in dating him.

She sure had left in a hurry, clearly disappointed in Brad, but she'd given him her phone number—so maybe it wasn't completely hopeless? Only, if he decided not to get involved in her cause, would she even want to see him again? He got that she felt strongly about this, in fact that was one of the things he liked about her, but it would be foolish to rush into trouble because of a crush.

Foolish, yes, but maybe it would be worth it. And not just to impress a girl. Brad had been looking for a purpose for a long time, more so since coming to college. He'd thought getting away from home and his parents would change his life, but so far it had only been a change of scenery. Brad wasn't satisfied with who he was and what he was doing. He wanted adventure, he wanted a fresh identity. He wanted to matter.

Perhaps Lee wasn't presenting Brad with a new problem, but with a new solution.

Brad's room was dark when he entered but for the flickering glow of Nick's TV on the right. Nick was usually watching bootleg tapes of shows or movies, but tonight there was something strange on the screen: a blue background with pixelated birds flapping across it. A video game? Nick was silhouetted against the screen, sitting in his bed with his back to the door.

"Hey, what's—" Brad began. Nick whirled to face him and pointed a gun at him. Brad flung his hands up and backpedaled as Nick pulled the trigger.

Click. The screen flashed, accompanied by a cartoony gunshot. The two blocky birds flew off the screen, and an animated dog emerged from behind a bush and laughed.

"I hate that dog," Nick said. He pointed his gun—now obviously a plastic toy—at the screen and unloaded another round into the dog, to no effect.

"Jesus," Brad said, his hand over his pounding heart.

"Gotcha," Nick said.

"I'm turning on the light." Brad flipped the switch, and Nick squinted and blinked. His blue Mohawk was wilting, and he had a couple of days' of beard growth. Takeout containers and piles of clothing littered the floor around his bed, delineating where his side of the room ended and Brad's began.

The gray toy gun was connected to a white-and-gray box on the floor. "What is that thing?" Brad asked.

A black cardboard box leaning against the Commodore 64 on Nick's desk had a big logo that read "Nintendo" with a picture of a robot and, in smaller letters, "Entertainment System."

"Nintendo? Those are the *Donkey Kong* guys."

"They just came out with this new home console," Nick said. More birds appeared on the screen, and Nick rapidly aimed, fired, and shot them down.

"What are you playing?" Brad sat on his bed, the metal frame creaking. He leaned toward the TV screen, mesmerized.

"It's called *Duck Hunt*." Nick fired again. *Click. Bang. Click. Bang. Click. Bang.*

"But it's rabbit season," Brad said.

"Don't start," Nick said.

"Where'd you get this?"

"FAO Schwarz. They have a big window display. These things aren't available anywhere else. Of course I had to buy one. It was only a hundred forty dollars."

Brad winced. He had seventy-five cents to his name, thanks to Lee. He couldn't imagine being able to blow a small fortune on an impulse buy.

Nick offered the toy gun to Brad. "You wanna try it?"

"Hell yeah." That was the nice thing about having a rich roommate. Brad got to play with all of Nick's expensive stuff. Brad bet they were one of the few dorm rooms on campus with a television, let alone a Betamax—and now video games. He'd really hit the jackpot, especially with everything Nick had been teaching him about computers and phreaking.

Brad took the gun. It was really easy to pick up and play, and it felt like an actual arcade shooter. Better even, because he didn't need to feed it quarters.

"So what have you been up to?" Nick asked.

"I found her," Brad said. He fired and missed a duck, but he got the next one.

"The girl from the protest?"

"Her name's Lee. Or I guess she found me."

As they traded off with the gun, Brad brought Nick up to speed on his conversation with Lee.

"So you're gonna do it, right?" Nick asked.

"Help her out? And risk being suspended or expelled or . . . grounded?"

"You're not helping her out, you're helping out South Africa. And . . . helping yourself out. Know whatahmean, know whatahmean, nudge nudge, know whatahmean, say no more?"

"It just seems so meaningless. We aren't going to make a difference, so why bother? They'll never know we even tried."

Nick pressed a button on the rectangular controller in his lap, and the game froze. "It's only meaningless if you're doing it to get some kind of credit, man. You'll know you tried, and maybe that's the important thing—so you can go on feeling like you did something, like there are decent people in the world and you're one of them."

Brad stared at Nick. He hadn't seen this side of his roommate before; he usually only got passionate about phreaking and computer stuff, tech toys like the Nintendo, and geeky movies.

"Not to mention, it'll help you get in her pants," Nick said.

"There. You ruined it," Brad said. "For a minute I was thinking you were sincere."

"I was, but our actions can have multiple purposes, and there's nothing wrong with that. We're all inherently selfish, aren't we? At least, that's what the Columbia Core teaches us."

"*Et tu*, Nick? I can't believe a guy who barely leaves his

computer is lecturing me on not doing enough."

"That doesn't mean I'm not trying to put some good out in the world. You can do a lot with computers, man. One day, the fight's going to be in cyberspace." He held up his beloved copy of *The Hacker's Handbook* and raised it over his head.

Brad rolled his eyes.

"You'll see. You can't halt the future. But for right now, you gotta get out there yourself to make the future what you want it to be."

"So you think I should help her."

"It's a moral imperative. Hell, I'll help too."

"Why?" Brad looked at Nick suspiciously. *What's his angle?*

"Sometimes it's fun just to mess with people too. Columbia makes a tempting target."

"What happened to putting good out in the world?" Brad asked.

"I'm a complex individual with warring impulses."

"Do you think you can do a micro thing, talk to their computer from here and get the information we need?" Brad asked.

"Of course I can. We're already on the same communications network. Trouble is, it could take months of work. I've already been working my way into their systems, but I haven't made much progress. Getting an admin password to the system, even access to someone's electronic mail account, would help things along. So you're right—this is going to have to be an in-person infiltration. Risky, but fun."

Brad shook his head.

"Look, if we get caught, we can pass this off as a prank or something. They expect us to be irresponsible and stupid."

"It *is* irresponsible and stupid." Yet in a way it was also taking responsibility in a way that Brad never had and most people never did. When the people in authority were themselves acting criminally or amorally, was it wrong to break their rules?

He'd told Lee that he was a model kid who never got in trouble, but that didn't mean he didn't break rules from time to time; he simply had never gotten caught. Shoplifting candy or sometimes books from stores, because he couldn't afford to buy them. Their family stealing cable TV to watch HBO. Getting free phone calls. Those were all definitely illegal, but no one was getting hurt really, and they were inherently selfish acts. This was different. It was completely selfless, and higher stakes.

Brad licked his lips. "All right. I'll consider it if we can come up with a plan that makes sense, with minimal risk."

Nick high-fived Brad. "Minimal risk, maximum fun."

Brad stood up. "I guess I'll call Lee and tell her the good news," he said.

"Hold on. You have to see what else the Nintendo can do. Look under your desk."

Brad pulled his chair out and looked under his desk. There was a small gray robot staring out at him.

"Jesus. You bought a robot too?"

"It came with the console. You use it to control this game." Nick held up a gray cartridge labeled *Gyromite*.

"Gee, that sounds fun. I'd rather play the game myself," Brad said.

"Stop trying to halt progress!" Nick said. "Now help me set up this contraption. It looks complicated."

It was *Gyromite* that gave Brad the idea of how they could safely get in and out of Hamilton Hall. Okay, maybe not "safely," but hopefully unseen.

The video game had the player navigate a sleepwalking professor through a deadly labyrinth of steel girders, dynamite, and gates. You used R.O.B., the "Robotic Operating Buddy," to raise and lower gates as the professor progressed through the level. The whole setup reminded Brad of some of the tunnels under Columbia University; though they weren't booby-trapped with dynamite as far as he knew, the steam tunnels and power conduits were just as dangerous, and some of the areas were potentially radioactive. Really.

Come to think of it, dynamite wasn't completely out of the question.

"The tunnels?" Nick said as they entered the Seeley W. Mudd building.

"Shh," Nick said. It was the middle of the afternoon, and he didn't want them to be overheard, even if the network of tunnels was an open secret. Some of them were available to students and still in use, ideal for getting from building to building on rainy or cold days. But those sections were limited, few and far between, and they hid a lower level of tunnels that were far more exciting, particularly if you were interested in illegal activities.

"Why Mudd?" Nick asked. "Isn't there a closer entrance? We're all the way on the other side of campus."

"Two reasons," Brad said. He pressed the Up button on the elevator, which got him another curious glance from Nick. "One, students have twenty-four-hour access to the building, unlike Hamilton, which is locked tight after business hours." The elevator dinged, and the doors opened. "And two, I have to pick something up first."

Brad spent a lot of time in Mudd for his computer science classes. He'd explored the building too, late at night. It was a surprisingly fun space; one of the labs even had a Ping-Pong table set up in a hallway. He'd also discovered he could get into places he wasn't supposed to, like a lab that was frequently left unlocked, where he could steal things like . . .

"Liquid nitrogen?!" Nick whispered. "What is that for?"

Brad had to admit, he liked surprising Nick for a change. He tucked the silver canister into a deep coat pocket and grinned. "You'll see."

Next they took the elevator down to the basement, then he accessed an unassuming door that led to an underused stairway that took them even deeper. In a large open space, a makeshift plywood wall fenced off a massive, strangely ominous machine.

"This is worth stopping for." Brad pointed to the crates stacked by the wall. "Climb up and take a look."

Nick grumbled, but he worked his way up the precarious pile. Brad watched Nick's face and wasn't disappointed: His roommate's jaw dropped and his eyes practically bugged out.

"Is that the cyclotron?" Nick asked.

"Close. It's a nuclear reactor Columbia built but never activated because of student protests a few years back." Brad paused. "Huh. I guess protesting can accomplish something after all."

Nick clambered back down and rubbed his hands on his jeans. "So the cyclotron is just an urban legend, then."

"No, it does exist, but it's over in Pupin. The whole lab from the Manhattan Project is basically untouched. I can take you over there sometime if you want." Brad was excited to be sharing this with Nick, after exploring the majority of the tunnels on his own, using information from other tunnel goers, the Columbia archives, and maps cobbled together and distributed through the BBS.

"I'll pass," Nick said. "Who are you? I had no idea you were doing all this."

"Good," Brad said. Tunnel exploring was the one definitively illegal thing he had done since coming to Columbia, but he wasn't harming anyone really. It seemed like the administration mostly looked the other way, and they had closed off a lot of access to limit students' movement. Or so they thought.

Coming down here with Nick, stealing lab materials, and planning to break into Hamilton to hack a computer was taking rule breaking to the next level. He was turning into quite a rebel.

"I like the tunnels," Brad said. "They're like a real-life version of *Zork*."

"I'd rather play *Zork*," Nick said. "Where to next?"

Brad led him to a door tucked away behind the dormant reactor. He knew it wasn't online, and there weren't any radioactive materials nearby—those were in Pupin too—but walking near it still gave him a tingly, unsettled feeling. Actually, it was kind of a turn-on. If anyone could understand that, with his love for machines and technology, it was Nick, but Brad didn't mention it.

Once they were in the tunnels proper, the air was stale and stifling, warm and wet. He smelled hot machine oil and cooking electronics. He supposed there might also be asbestos and mold.

"Uh, try not to breathe." Brad pulled his T-shirt collar up over his nose and mouth.

"Awesome," Nick said, following suit.

The next stretch was fairly straightforward as Brad guided Nick south on campus, beneath Schermerhorn Hall, then beneath Fayerweather. He had to hunt around for the access point that would take him farther; it was so well hidden, he'd only found it before by the grace of a maintenance worker.

It was risky to come down here during the daytime, when staff might be about. Brad had once seen one of them down here late at night. They had looked at each other quietly for a moment, before the man nodded toward the corner and moved on. That's how Brad had found the hidden door that let him continue on his way.

The other tunnel explorers who had preceded him had labeled this route as a rumor, but they often phrased their hints as obscure clues, making Brad work for the solution before discovering the treasure. He didn't mind, but he was happy to have the unexpected help after many frustrating nights trying to find the way.

In retrospect, that guy may not have worked for the university at all; he could have been another tunnel explorer like Brad. Maybe people even lived down here, like C.H.U.D.s.

Under Saint Paul's they hit their first real barrier: a padlocked chain with thick steel links threaded through the handles of ancient double doors. Looking at the rusted hinges, he wasn't sure he could open them even if he got the lock off.

"Where are we now?" Nick huffed. He wiped sweat from his brow.

It was sweltering down here, with boiler pipes and electrical conduits running alongside most of the narrow passageways. Some of them emitted steam periodically, but if you listened for the distant clanging sound that signaled the impending release, you could steer clear of the spurts of hot vapor. It was all a marvel of engineering, another of those complex systems that could be so easily sabotaged by the human element. Turn a valve here, cut a cable there, and they could make things uncomfortable for a lot of people without anyone aboveground realizing it.

"We're under the chapel," Brad said.

"Hey, you think this leads to a crypt?" Nick suddenly sounded more eager than he had about the cyclotron.

"I doubt it. At least, I don't think so." Brad removed the liquid nitrogen and put on a thick glove.

"You're kidding," Nick said.

"This is as far as I've gotten, because of this damn lock. By the time anyone discovers it's broken, hopefully we'll be long gone."

Brad very carefully unscrewed the lid of the thermos and poured the contents over the lock. The metal quickly frosted over and steamed. Brad waited a moment before he bashed the metal thermos against it: once, twice, three times, and the lock cracked and opened. He used his mittened hand to pull it off and set it aside.

"Open says me," Brad said as he dragged the door open. It stuck, but he and Nick put all their weight into it together, and it screamed open, inch by inch, rust flaking off and drifting down like orange-brown snow.

It felt like they were opening Al Capone's secret vault under the Lexington Hotel. He knew other students had been through here before him—he had their scattered, sometimes contradictory, often cryptic notes, of course—but it was still the first time he'd done this himself. Part of him felt like a poseur when he used phone-phreaking exploits and other hacks, because he was relying on things other, smarter people had come up with, but it was also thrilling to make use of them himself, to try new things. He had been getting a more eccentric, but more satisfying education at Columbia than he had expected.

Brad shined his flashlight into the darkness.

"You know, we're going to a lot of trouble to sneak into Hamilton. What if we just hide in a bathroom or something until the building is locked up?" Nick said.

"Don't tell me you're afraid of the dark," Brad said.

"I'm not afraid. I just don't like it very much."

"Let's keep going. I promise we won't be eaten by a grue." Brad shoved a brick in the door to keep it propped open and marched on into an even narrower crawl space.

Brad got turned around a couple of times, and they had to backtrack to find the route that led to the next adjoining building, Philosophy. Then they made their way to Kent.

"'A maze of twisty little passages, all alike,'" Nick muttered. "I hope you can find our way back."

"The only way out is through," Brad said. "If we do this right, we'll get into Hamilton."

Right now they were crossing under College Walk. At the end of a corridor packed with pipes and cables, which brushed against his shoulders as he passed between them, was another door. This one had an old Master Lock pitted with rust. He tried pulling the door open, but it was stuck fast. A metal sign in its center read THIS DOOR IS TO REMAIN LOCKED AT ALL TIMES.

"No more liquid nitrogen," Nick observed.

"I have a tool for this one." Brad pulled out a paper clip, stretched it out into a long wire, and bent it into a U shape. He twisted one end into a tiny hook.

"You pick locks too?"

"We'll see. I have instructions on how to do this one lock, but I've never tried before."

He knelt on the warm, damp concrete floor and focused on the lock. Beside it, in black permanent marker, someone had scribbled "Frodo Lives!"

It took thirty-three minutes, but eventually Brad opened the door, more by dumb luck than skill, he thought. Whatever, the results were what mattered.

"Why can't you just pick the locks on the main entrance to the building?" Nick asked.

"It just took me half an hour to open a lock with instructions," Brad said. "We'd be caught, plus they'd see us on the security cameras. And we have to do more than just get into the building."

They entered a small room, more of a closet really, with a wall of exposed cables of many colors and thicknesses. Nick's eyes lit up. "Communications junction," he said. "Now we're talking."

There was another door on the opposite wall, which was fortunately unlocked.

Nick opened it and leaned out. "Weird. There's a thick forest outside. It's snowing heavily, but I think . . . I can make out a lamppost in the distance."

Brad laughed. He pushed Nick aside and poked his head out the door. They were behind a dark stairwell leading up. A broken vending machine was tucked into the corner. He heard bustling activity upstairs as students talked and walked to their classes. He eased the door closed.

"We made it!" he said.

"Great," Nick said. "Now what?"

"In 1968, when student protesters held this building, kids from the campus radio station, WKCR, tapped the phone lines so they could monitor calls and police activity."

Nick nodded. "I knew that."

"Are you up for a little historical reenactment?" Brad asked. "So we can get some intel on President Sovern? We need to know when he's going to leave, stuff about his personal life."

"That'll be useful in guessing his password too, if we need to," Nick said.

"Maybe if we're lucky, we'll hear him talking to a trustee about the school's investments. That kind of thing."

"So that's why you asked me to bring this stuff." Nick started pulling out an assortment of clippers and wires and boxes and a large black phone handset with a cord and plug from the pockets of his long black overcoat. He'd insisted on wearing it, even though it was hot and harder to navigate in the tunnels with it on.

Now that he was back in his element, his natural arrogance came out. "Unless they've taken precautions since the strike in the sixties, this should be a piece of cake." He shrugged. "Eh, it should be easy anyway. I've been breaking into trunk lines since I was eleven."

"Everyone needs a hobby," Brad said.

Nick sniffed. "This isn't a *hobby*. It's a calling. Now get out of my way. I have miracles to work."

The next afternoon, Brad walked into President Sovern's office in Hamilton Hall carrying a black duffel bag. He checked the pens in his pocket protector and felt his heart pounding beneath it. He wiped his sweaty palms on his jeans and approached the receptionist's desk. She was busy on her typewriter, transcribing scribbles from a yellow legal pad. Brad waited patiently until she glanced up with an irritated expression.

"Can I help you?" she asked.

"I'm from ADP. Um, Administrative Data Processing?"

She raised her eyebrows.

"Um, President Sovern called about a problem with his Ethernet connection," Brad said.

She frowned. "I'm sorry, you just missed him."

I know, Brad thought. He and Nick had been listening to Sovern's calls from their wiretap in the basement. Thirty minutes ago he had called his wife to remind her about their guests for dinner, an alumnus of the college and his wife—potential donors. Ten minutes ago his secretary had called various campus offices to make sure they were ready for a tour Sovern was personally leading. They'd waited a few more minutes, and then Brad walked upstairs and into the office.

"That's okay, he doesn't need to be there," Brad said.

"He didn't say you'd be coming in. Can this wait until the morning?" she asked.

Brad really started to sweat. "If I don't fix this right away, I'll get in trouble. The last time President Sovern couldn't get his electronic mail, we got hell for it. You know how he is."

She pressed her lips together. Brad didn't know how Sovern was, aside from how he came off in articles in the *Columbia Spectator*—like your average bureaucrat. Nick had told him to make this play though, on the assumption that having a boss who was a pain in the ass was a universal constant.

"He does love electronic mail," she said. "But I can't—"

Her phone rang. Brad glanced at his watch. Right on time, Lee.

"Hold on a moment." She picked up the handset and answered. "President Sovern's office. How can I help you?" She listened for a moment, and her eyes drifted back to Brad. "Yes, he's here right now. I understand. Yes, it's so hard to keep up with all this paperwork! All right. All right. Thanks. You too."

Brad didn't know what script Lee had been going from, but it seemed to have worked.

The woman stood up. "That was your supervisor's assistant calling. They're still working on the proper forms, but apparently President Sovern called it in on his way out—and didn't bother telling me. He has so much going on today, I'm sure it slipped his mind. I suppose it's okay for you to work on his computer as long as you aren't in there alone."

Brad's spirits fell, but he kept smiling. "Sure, sure. Shouldn't take long."

She opened a drawer and pulled out a key ring. Then she walked around her desk and led him toward the mahogany double doors leading into the office. As she slid the key into the lock, the outer door opened again, and Nick sauntered in.

"Hello?" he called loudly.

A look of annoyance passed over the assistant's face as she took in Nick's freshly spiked Mohawk, pierced ear, sloppy T-shirt, torn jeans, and Chucks. "I'll be right with you." She looked at Brad. "Wait right here."

Brad slipped a hand into his pocket. The little ball of Silly Putty warmed in his palm. "Sorry, I need to wrap this up. It's my last call for the day, and the boss doesn't like me doing over-time."

"Hey!" Nick called. "Can I get some service over here?"

She looked back and forth between Brad and Nick. She pocketed the keys. "Fine. I'll just be a moment."

"I'll be done before you know it," Brad said.

She headed back to her desk, where Nick was doing what he did best: acting obnoxious. He leaned over her typewriter and read what she'd been writing.

With one eye on the woman arguing with Nick over what-ever ridiculous demand he was placing on her, Brad mashed up the sticky wad of clay and crammed it into the strike plate in the doorjamb. He grimaced when he saw how obvious the coral-colored substance was, but he pushed it in with his thumb—

shit, fingerprints!—then smoothed over the excess. She glanced over at him just as he finished.

Nick snapped his fingers in front of her face. "Over here, ma'am."

What an asshole, Brad thought. At least it was mostly for distraction.

He slipped into the office and checked the computer. It was an IBM PC, just like Nick said it'd be. He knew all about the different machines installed on campus and where they all were.

Brad hesitated. He wasn't familiar with this model. He didn't even have his own computer; he had to do all his work on the Superbrain microcomputers in the student labs, or sometimes Nick would let him use his PC. He'd have to learn more about the IBM computers before they came back later, but for now, he knew what he needed to do. He followed the thick yellow Ethernet cable from the back of the computer to a port in the wall. He unplugged it and then went back to the desk—just in time.

The assistant was back. "It's almost time to lock up the office," she said. "How's it coming?"

"Nearly done." Brad stood up again and walked back over to the wall port. "Yup, just as I thought. Here's the problem." He picked up the loose cable and showed it to her. "These are so easy to pull out of the wall without noticing it when you walk by or kick under the desk with your feet." He plugged it back in and returned to the computer.

He switched on the monitor, and when it brightened, he

saw the machine was locked. He didn't have the password, but he clicked a few keys on the keyboard and then nodded. "All better."

He switched off the monitor. "Thanks for your help." He stepped into the outer office. Nick was gone.

Brad pulled the door shut behind him, to minimize the chance that she would notice the putty in the door. He hoped she'd forget to lock it, but no such luck. As she turned the key, he blurted out, "Hey, would you like some coffee?"

"It's almost three o'clock." She glanced at the door and frowned. She'd noticed it hadn't felt right when the lock turned. "If I drink coffee now, I'll be up all night."

"That could be a good thing," Brad said.

Brad hated the words coming out of his mouth, but they did the trick. She slid the key out of the lock and looked him over.

"What's your name again?" she asked.

"Chris Knight." Brad winked. Ugh, that might be pushing it a bit. He rubbed at his eye as if something was in it.

"What are you suggesting, Chris?"

"Well, your boss isn't here, so there's no harm in leaving a little early, right? So I thought you might like to have coffee. With me. But we could go for caffeine-free drinks, if you'd prefer." He smiled.

"No, thank you," she said. "I think I'd rather call your supervisor to report your unprofessional behavior." She crossed her arms.

Brad's eyes widened. "Please don't do that! I'm sorry! I

didn't mean to insult you. It was supposed to be a compliment. You're very attractive."

He was pretending to be upset, but it actually would mess up their plans if she called ADP and found out that they had no employees named Chris Knight.

"Oh, I see." She appeared to relax. "So I should be grateful."

"Of course not! But please don't call my supervisor. I need my job," Brad said.

"I need mine too. That's why I can't leave early. But we close the office at five. . . ." She raised her eyebrows.

"I can come back then," Brad said. *Is this real life?*

"You do that. Make it ten after, just to be safe."

"Dinner?" Brad asked. Crap. He'd have to borrow some money from Nick or Lee. Well, that could be awkward.

"I like to eat," she said. "See you then."

Brad left the office. He checked the strike plate on his way out—Nick had filled that one too, while she'd been in the president's office with Brad.

Lee was waiting outside Hamilton Hall. She was sitting reading a book, but when he came through the doors, she jumped up and rushed over.

"Did you do it?"

Brad nodded. "It was easier than I expected." His pulse was still racing. He'd been nervous about getting caught or failing to do what he had to, but it had also been exciting. The real test would be tonight, of course.

Nick emerged from the building. He smiled when he saw Brad. "You're fired."

"What?" Brad asked.

"As your fake manager at ADP, Paul Atreides, I'm going to have to let you go for sexual harassment of a university employee."

"Uh," Brad said.

"What?" Lee asked.

"Romeo here made a very bad pass at President Sovern's personal assistant, who called his boss immediately after he left. Fortunately, I was in the basement monitoring calls from the office, and I intercepted her complaint."

"Brad?" Lee frowned. "That wasn't part of the plan." She actually seemed . . . jealous. She absently ruffled the pages of her paperback book with a thumb, one finger holding her place.

"I was only trying to distract her so she wouldn't realize I'd stuck something in the lock. I had to improvise. It worked, at least."

"Only because you insulted her and pissed her off," Nick said. He stared at Brad and then laughed. "Hold the phone. Did you think she was really into you?"

"No!" Brad's face turned red.

Lee giggled.

"Maybe. I can't believe she ratted me out. I thought we made a connection there," Brad said.

"She's a better actor than you are," Nick said. "Fortunately your job is fake. Did you get into Sovern's computer?"

"It has a password," Brad said.

"*Pffpt*," Nick said. "That'll be easier than the doors."

"I wish I had your optimism," Brad said.

"Even if we can't get into the computer, they're bound to have paper files." Lee grabbed Brad's arm. "This is great! Thank you so much, Brad. You too. It's Nick, right?"

"He's my roommate," Brad said.

"Brad told me about you. You're a hacker," Lee said.

"Shhhh . . . ," Nick said. "By the way, you have superior taste in books." He pulled a book from his back pocket and held it out. She was startled. It was a more-worn copy of the book she had in her hands: *Neuromancer* by William Gibson.

"Book twins!" she said.

Nick had been bugging him to read that since they had moved in. Now Brad regretted not getting around to it, but he barely had time to read stuff for class. *The Iliad* was not light reading.

"This is my second time reading it," Lee said. "It's so fascinating."

"I agree. I've read it fifteen times already. Hey, you should come hang out with us in our room until we do the job. Since Brad's date is canceled and all. Have you seen *Red Dawn*?"

Lee sighed. "I'd love to, but I have to go to a play tonight. My father basically sponsored it, so attendance is not optional. I can get extra tickets though, if either of you is interested. I can't promise it will be as exciting as repelling a Soviet invasion on American soil." She paused. "In fact, it's pretty boring. I read the script."

Nick yawned exaggeratedly. "Not me. I missed my after-noon siesta, and I'd better get some sleep if we're going to be out late tonight."

Lee looked at Brad hopefully.

"What's it called?" he asked.

"*Things Are Not Okay*," she said. "It's about the end of a marriage."

Brad stifled a yawn of his own. He shrugged. "Yeah, why not? Theater's one of the benefits of living in New York, right?"

Yes! he thought.

Nick grinned at him. "Sounds like the perfect date. Take in a show, then commit burglary. Have fun, kids."

Lee blushed.

"Let's meet back here at midnight." Brad handed his bag to Nick. "Take this back to our room? I'll swing by and pick you up when it's time for the real show to start."

Apparently Brad needed a nap too. He kept falling asleep during the play, until Lee would nudge him with her elbow and he'd startle awake. After intermission, she grabbed his hand—and he'd had no trouble staying awake from then on.

This is totally a date! he thought.

But it was a weird first date, with her parents sitting just on her other side in their private box. Her mother occasionally sneaked glances down the row at Brad, but her father acted like he wasn't even there, totally focused on the play.

Brad didn't mind; after all, in only a few hours they were going to break into President Sovern's office to find information that would potentially make the trustees—including Mr. Monroe—look very bad. He didn't even know the man, and Brad felt guilty. He couldn't imagine how Lee felt about the prospect.

When the show ended, Mr. Monroe turned to face his daughter and Brad. Brad hastily pulled his hand from Lee's.

"Did you enjoy the play, Bradley?" Mr. Monroe asked.

"Yes, sir," Brad said.

"You snore," Lee whispered.

"It was, uh, very refreshing," Brad said. Lee rolled her eyes at him.

Mr. Monroe laughed. "I'm always happy to see young people take an interest in the arts. We have to drag Lianna to these things now. The only way she agreed to come tonight is if we bribed her with cheesecake after the show."

"Lianna says you met at school. I thought we knew all her classmates. Are you in a club together?" Mrs. Monroe asked.

Brad smiled. Lee had totally nailed her mother's British accent.

"Sort of," Lee said.

"Do we know your parents?" Mr. Monroe asked. "We must. But I don't recall meeting any Steins. What do they do?"

"I doubt you would have heard of them," Brad said. "I'm from California."

"Oh." Mr. Monroe frowned. "What business are they in?"

"Dad's in construction, and Mom's in real estate." Brad's father was a carpenter, and his mother was a Realtor.

"Would you like to join us for dessert, Bradley?" Mrs. Monroe asked. "It would be nice to get to know you a little better."

"Now, Glenda. There's no need to pry," Mr. Monroe said. "A man likes his privacy."

I'm sure you do, Brad thought.

"No, I'd love to—" Brad began.

"But he has too much homework to finish. Don't you, Brad?" Lee said.

He stared at her. From hand-holding to trying to get rid of him in less than five minutes. He just didn't get her sometimes.

"Of course! I forgot, it's a school night," Mrs. Monroe said.

Lee laughed, but it seemed kind of forced. "Oh, Mother!" she cackled.

"I'll call you a taxi," Mr. Monroe said.

"Thanks, but I'm okay on the subway," Brad said. Who could afford to take cabs everywhere in New York?

Mrs. Monroe's brow furrowed. "Do be careful."

"Sure. Thank you for a wonderful evening. I guess I'll see you later, Lee." Brad stood up.

"Good night, Brad. Thanks for coming." Now she was all formal. She wouldn't even look at him. He was getting the impression that she wanted to get rid of him. Was she embarrassed because he wasn't from a good family like hers? Or worried he'd spill something about their plans?

At least he didn't have to worry about trying to move in for the kiss, or worrying if it was appropriate, with her mother and father right there and Lee suddenly so cool to him. Maybe she'd just realized how far apart their worlds were, or he had been misreading her as badly as he had the receptionist that afternoon.

Still, when Brad looked at Lee and her parents, now chattering about parts of the play he'd slept through, he suddenly had a strange thought: *This is going to be my family one day.*

"Getting a little ahead of yourself, eh, tiger?" Nick said. "You just met her. And her parents." He shook his head.

They were once again standing outside of the Mudd building, but this time they were waiting for Lee to show up. She was ten minutes late.

"You see how awesome she is, right?" Brad hefted his bag on his shoulder, now heavier with its load of tools for their break-in. He had no idea what they'd really need, but he figured it was better to be overprepared.

"She's pretty cute. Very . . . intense." Nick grinned. "Don't screw this up."

"Thanks," Brad said.

"You're certainly going to a lot of trouble for her."

"It's not for her. Not just for her. Not anymore."

"That almost sounded convincing. Keep working on it," Nick said.

Lee came hurrying up. "I'm sorry I'm late. I had trouble sneaking out. And I'm sorry about before. I'm sure that was a little awkward," she said.

By unspoken agreement, they were all wearing black. Nick had on a Black Sabbath T-shirt and black sweatpants. Brad had on a black button-down shirt and black suit pants. Lee was wearing a black hoodie, black tights, and black leg warmers.

"Nah, it was perfectly normal. That's how all my dates go," Brad said.

"You go on a lot of dates?" she asked.

Nick laughed. "He doesn't. At all. That's why his statement is true."

"Hey," Brad said. "Why did I invite you?"

"Because I'm the brains of this operation. You're the beauty, of course." Nick nodded at Lee.

"What about me?" Brad asked.

"You're the comic relief."

"Hold on. *I'm* the brains," Lee said. "Brad's the beauty."

Brad was grateful that it was too dark for her to see him blush.

Nick raised an eyebrow. "And I'm?"

"The third wheel." She stuck out her tongue.

"Well, then I guess you don't need me to be the lookout," Nick said.

"Lookout?" Brad asked. "You aren't coming with us?"

Nick gestured with his eyes to Lee and shook his head slightly.

"Once through those tunnels was enough for me," Nick said. "I prefer to stay aboveground, thanks very much."

"I thought you'd feel at home in a basement," Brad said.

"Watch it, nerd."

"I'll meet you guys back at Hamilton," Nick said.

"Tunnels?" Lee asked. "Did I miss something? I was wondering why you wanted to meet all the way up here. I've never been to this building before."

"I thought every Columbia student knew about the tunnels by now," Brad said. "They even covered it on my campus tour."

"I must have missed it."

He explained about the tunnels and why they had to enter them from Mudd and backtrack to Hamilton while Nick opened Brad's duffel bag. Nick pulled out two walkie-talkies with a green-and-gray-camouflage pattern.

He handed one to Brad. "We'll stay in touch with these. If I see anyone enter Hamilton, I'll warn you. We probably should have cased out the place to figure out what the security guards' schedule is, but . . ." He shrugged. "This is more interesting."

"Oh, there's one more thing," Brad said. He reached into the bag and pulled out a rubber Halloween mask. He handed it to Lee.

She held it up and giggled. "A gorilla!"

Brad handed one to Nick.

"I'm not wearing that. Don't you think it'll be more suspicious if masked students are caught inside the building after hours?"

"No reason we can't have a little fun with it." Brad pulled

his mask over his head. The small eyeholes limited his view, and it was stifling under there. His breath immediately started to make the inside of it slick with condensation, and it stank about as much as he figured a real gorilla did.

"These aren't practical at all," he said.

Lee pulled her mask off. "No, but I love that you thought of them. I'm keeping mine, and we can wear them at the Village Halloween Parade."

Brad caught himself grinning because it sounded like she was already making plans for them after this caper was over. Fortunately, his idiotic expression was hidden by the mask. He composed himself and tugged it off. Then he tucked it back into the bag with Lee's.

Brad's walkie-talkie crackled. "Good luck, guys. Over." Nick's voice blared through the speaker and echoed right beside Brad.

"You're right in front of us," Brad said. "You don't need the walkie-talkie."

Nick cupped a hand over his ear and tilted his head toward Brad. He shook his head. He held up his walkie-talkie.

Brad sighed. He pressed the Talk button and repeated, "We don't need these yet."

"Just want to make sure it's working. Over."

Brad sighed. "Dork. Over."

Lee laughed. "This is going to be the best night ever."

"I'll remind you that you said that in an hour," Brad said.

Lee took to the tunnels a lot better than Nick had. She had

an adventurous spirit. By the time they reached Hamilton's subbasement, in a record time of thirty-five minutes, they had another tentative activity lined up: She definitely wanted to see the cyclotron, and she wanted to add their names to the Signature Room in the steam tunnels along the west side of campus. She wanted to do these things—*with him*. He couldn't wait to explore them, and hopefully much more, with her. Maybe a life of crime wasn't so bad if you had the right partner.

When they entered the communications junction under Hamilton, Lee grinned and clapped her hands softly.

"Are you slow-clapping me?" Brad asked.

"I'm not being sarcastic—I'm trying to be quiet. I'm seriously impressed, Brad. You aren't just a pretty face. That whole trip was amazing!"

"Now that's a compliment. Or is it?" Brad lifted his walkie-talkie. "We're in, Nick. Over."

He took a look around to make sure Nick had removed all traces of their wiretap, then they headed upstairs. Brad had brought flashlights, but the halls were still lit normally, which made them somehow more eerie than if it were dark. They took the elevator up to the third floor, and the moment of truth came. Brad held the knob of the door to the president's office, turned it—and it opened.

"So far so good," he said. He carefully teased the Silly Putty out of the lock mechanism, rolled it into a ball, and threw it up to the ceiling, where it stuck fast.

"A waste of perfectly good Silly Putty," Lee said.

"It served its purpose, and there's more where that came from." He swept his arm forward. "After you."

She bowed and then stepped inside, with him following close behind.

The office inside was dark. Brad pulled out the flashlights and handed one to Lee. "Better keep the lights off," he said.

"How Nancy Drew," she said.

"I guess that makes me Nick and the Hardy Boys?" Brad said.

She spotted the file cabinets lining the far side of the office and went, "Oooh." She made a beeline for them.

"Okay. I'll check the president's computer," Brad said. "What are we looking for?"

"Anything about the trustees, especially minutes of their meetings from the spring until now. Financial records and letters about investments. Anything that looks juicy."

"Juicy. So I'll know it when I see it," Brad said.

"I guess . . ." She was already opening drawers and pawing through file folders.

Brad went to the inner office door and encountered their first hiccup: It wouldn't open.

"Shit," he said. Maybe the secretary had found the putty after all, or it hadn't been enough to keep the lock from latching.

He jiggled the handle in frustration. He went back to the assistant's desk and tried the drawer she'd stored the keys in. Locked.

This lock appeared to be easier to pick, or certainly break, than the one on the door—but if he caused any damage, it would be immediately clear that someone had broken in. And he bet she'd connect the dots to either him or Nick, or both.

Instead, he went back to the president's door and started jiggling the doorknob and pushing and pulling.

"Should you be making that much noise?" Lee asked.

"The door's locked," he said.

"Try a credit card."

"I don't have a credit card!" he said.

"Should we abort the mission?" she asked.

"No, hold on . . ." He pulled out his student ID and inserted it between the door and the frame, jiggling it around the lock. The card finally slid home, and he pulled it back gently, easing the lock back. He grabbed the handle and yanked the door open. "Got it. Carry on," he said.

"It worked! Nice going," Lee said.

He swept the flashlight over the room. It definitely looked more sinister than it had earlier that day. The potted fern in the corner made shadows creep along the walls like a grotesque dark hand reaching out.

There was a credenza and a tall bookshelf stuffed with leather-bound volumes. A large cabinet TV was situated in front of a burgundy sofa, like someone's living room had been transplanted there. And there was the desk, a massive piece of furniture with the computer perched on one end, to the right of the giant reclining office chair.

Brad sat down in the chair, swiveled around in it once, twice.

Then he switched on the monitor and saw the password-lock screen he'd faced before.

He pressed the walkie-talkie. "Nick, we're in. I'm staring at the guy's computer. You have some trick for getting past the password?"

He waited a long time. Sighed. "Over," he added.

"Good. Before you do anything else, look around for a slip of paper with the password on it. It might be in a drawer, or hidden in a book or something."

Brad lifted the keyboard. "Or under the keyboard," he said.

"Good thought."

"No, that's where it is." Brad shone the flashlight on a yellow sticky note with a word scrawled in pen: HAMILTON.

"Wow," Brad said. He typed the letters into the password screen and was greeted with the DOS prompt.

C:/

"That did it," Brad said. "What an idiot."

"I told you it would be easy. Frankly, I'm surprised it had a password at all."

Brad typed, "DIR-W," and the directory listing scrolled. He squinted at the glowing white letters on the black screen. He'd been hoping for a file folder named "SECRET," but no such luck. This was all the usual boring stuff you'd expect to find on any-one's computer, though there was one enticing-looking direc-tory named "novel."

"I think this is a dead end," Brad said.

"Try looking for hidden folders," Nick said.

"Right. Uh, can you walk me through that?" Brad asked.

Nick rattled off a series of commands—letters and strokes and dashes and slashes. Brad tried to keep up, the keyboard sounding like little gunshots in the cavernous office each time he pressed a key. From the next room, he heard the methodical sound of file drawers scraping open, paper rustling, and then the soft shush-click of them closing again.

"He might not keep this stuff on his own micro," Nick said. "I wonder if you can connect to the financial records in Hogan from there."

"Thanks for this," Brad whispered. "Helping me look good, I mean."

"This is the strangest Cyrano de Bergerac shit I've ever heard of," Nick said. "It's like hacking a person. I like a good challenge."

"Huh, I never thought of it that way," Brad said. He felt a little guilty that he couldn't do this stuff without Nick's help, but he would learn it all one day for real.

He also thought Nick might be right. If you applied the same logic that Perrow did to technological systems, and the human flaws in them, as the world became more connected with the ARPANET and networking, computers were going to be a huge tool in securing—and stealing—sensitive information. As security measures improved, it would become easier to hack people to get access to those systems.

Brad heard a new sound from the outer office. A humming and whirring that sounded as loud as a jet engine. A pulsing light flashed inside the room. He got up and poked his head out.

"What's going on?" he whispered.

"I'm making copies on this Xerox machine," Lee said.

"You found something?" Brad asked.

"I think so. I'm just going to take the whole folder and go through it later."

He chewed his lip. "Why bother? Just take the originals. Either way, they'll know someone was here once we release them."

"That's stealing, Brad."

"I think I'm missing some nuance of what we're doing here."

"How about you? Find anything?"

"Nothing on the computer so far. I think we're gonna try his electronic mail account next."

"Good," she said distractedly, reading over pages as they came out of the photocopying machine.

Brad sat back down and called up telnet. He figured the president's username was just like everyone else's, initials plus a number, but since the system was new, it was just mis@columbia.edu. And the password . . .

"It can't be the same," Brad muttered as he typed, "HAMILTON."

It was the same.

"Newsflash," he told Nick through the walkie-talkie. "Same password for his mail."

"You don't say. Noted," Nick replied.

And here's where all the good stuff was. The president

wasn't very organized, so all his messages were still in his inbox: hundreds of them already since the account had been created only a few months before. He really did love electronic mail.

Brad sorted the messages by subject and found a chunk of them with the subject line: "RE: S.A. Finances." He recognized some of the addressees as members of the Columbia board of trustees, including one name in particular. Brad opened one message from <Monroe, Aloysius> monroe@pnp.com and skimmed its contents.

> I concur with Harry and Gerald that we should make a superficial effort that appears to divest from our South African interests. To appease the protestors and moralists, with whom I share sympathy. While personally I have made it a priority to separate myself and my business from South African affairs, it is my opinion that it would be devastating to the University if we disengaged from our key holdings—in this current economic climate. As harmful as this negative attention has been and damaging to business, I have no doubt that the current furor will die down, it already has begun! Naturally over the next few years we can revisit our portfolio and redistribute according to the changing political winds.

Brad sucked in a breath. Mr. Monroe had seemed like a nice guy after the play, but he was also selfish and greedy and unethical. How could you reconcile those opposing qualities in a

person? Were people always performing, pretending to be someone else? How could you ever know who someone truly was?

Brad already knew the answer to that: You had to judge a
person's character by their actions alone. But that left him with
a new question: What kind of person did he want to be?

Brad's first instinct was to delete this message so Lee
wouldn't see it, but if anyone deserved to know the truth, it was
her, right? And how would it look if she released this information but conveniently protected her own father's role in the decision to lie about divesting from South Africa?

Brad also considered closing the electronic mail program
and telling her that he hadn't managed to find anything useful.
That would be the easiest thing for everyone, but it would be a
lie covering up another lie. . . .

What do I do?

Well, Lee had made her decision. It wasn't up to Brad to
protect her from it. This might just be a case of being careful
what you wish for.

He hit the Print key. From the far side of the office came
mechanical whirs and clicks as the printer stirred to life. Then
the irritating, high-pitched screech as it began committing the
electronic messages to paper, one line at a time. It was going to
take forever to print all these out.

Lee came running in with an armful of folders. "What the
hell is that?" she asked.

"Printer." Brad stood and walked toward the credenza. He
opened a cabinet door, and the sound got louder. A long strip of

paper was feeding into the gray-and-white printer and stacking into folded pages behind it.

"So much for keeping a low profile," she said.

"Someone would have to already be in the hallway to hear us, and at that point we're screwed," Brad said.

"What did you find?" she asked.

"I'm not sure." Brad looked away. "Some electronic mail messages about the university's investments in South African companies. Recommendations from the board. That kind of thing. I thought I should print them out so you can read through them all later. And in case they delete the messages to cover their tracks."

"Couldn't you just forward copies to another electronic mail account?" Lee asked.

Brad smacked his forehead. "That's a much better idea."

He went back to the computer and highlighted all the messages to forward them to another account as one large text file. "What's your electronic mail address?" he asked.

He was already typing *lmonroe@columbia.edu* when she said, "I don't have one."

"You haven't used yours yet? That's okay, they—"

"No. Brad, I don't have my own electronic mail."

"But the university gives one to every student."

She chewed her lip, and finally Brad got it.

"You don't go here," he said.

She shook her head slowly, looking contrite.

"You've been pretending to be a Columbia student? Why? Where do you go? NYU?"

"Spence," she said.

"I don't know that one. Is it in Westchester?"

"It's private. I'm in the upper school."

"Upper school. You mean . . . *high school*? You're in high school?! How old are you?"

"Sixteen," she said.

Brad opened his mouth. He had nothing to say. Or rather, none of the things he wanted to say were appropriate. Finally, something came to mind.

"But . . . *why*?" he asked.

"You already asked me that."

"And you didn't answer."

"I wanted to get involved. Columbia was the main focus, so it seemed the most likely place to start. But campus groups don't usually welcome students from other schools, let alone secondary schools. . . . No one ever asked, you know? I just started showing up, and they were glad to have me."

"You did more than show up. You practically took over the group."

She sniffed. "You do what you must to get results."

Brad stared at the screen, grateful for the excuse not to look her in the eyes. She was only a couple of years younger than him, and it shouldn't make any difference in his feelings for her. And yet the distance between high school and college seemed significant, even if he'd only just entered college himself.

She seemed much older though, and she'd already accomplished a lot more with her life than he had. Until today. If he really thought about it, she'd been a better Columbia student than he had so far. She was involved and engaged; he was the one who felt like he was pretending he belonged there.

"Brad?" Lee asked. For the first time since he'd met her, she sounded unsure of herself.

"Yeah," he said.

"We can talk about all this later, okay? You need to focus so we can get out of here."

"Yeah," he repeated. He went back to work.

Brad didn't want to send these electronic mail messages to his own account, but it ought to be safe if he covered his tracks and deleted the sent mail when he was done. He went ahead and started. You do what you must to get results.

Lee's father's name blipped across his screen again as it was added to the file being forwarded to his account.

"Lee, did you decide to do all this because of your father?" he asked.

She sat on the edge of the desk. "It was kind of personal. I wasn't doing it to piss him off or anything. But once I knew the board wasn't on the up-and-up, I had to look into it. If he found out what I was doing . . . when he finds out, I think he'll be proud of me. He's big on justice."

Brad made a noncommittal noise deep in his throat. He doubted Mr. Monroe was going to be proud of his daughter exposing his complicity in the university's deception. Hell, Mr. Monroe had almost suggested it himself!

"You could have told me who you were," Brad said.

Lee frowned. "I did. My age, where I go to school, who I'm related to . . . None of those things matter. The protests"—she swept her arms wide and looked around the office—"this is who I am."

"Yeah, but I thought . . . I mean, I'm . . ."

Lee blushed. "Me too. All the more reason not to tell you I'm still in high school. But don't worry, I was going to. I would have, if . . . when . . . before . . ."

Now it was Brad's turn to blush.

The mail program dinged. Saved by the bell. He checked to make sure the block of messages had been sent, then he deleted the record from the outbox. He canceled the ongoing print job and logged out of the program and shut down the computer.

A minute later, the printer went silent, and the room seemed deathly quiet. Until he heard the low squawk of the walkie-talkie from the credenza, where he'd left it.

"Mayday, Mayday," Nick whispered.

Lee and Brad stared at each other. She snatched up the unit. "What's wrong?" she asked.

"Jesus, what the hell were you two doing? Never mind, I can guess. I've been sounding the alarm for two minutes."

"The alarm?" Lee asked.

"A security guard just entered the building!" Nick said.

"Damn it!" Lee looked at the door. "How much time do we have, Nick?"

"I don't know. Two minutes less than you would have if you'd heard me calling you earlier."

Brad took the walkie from Lee. "Grab everything you found and hide any trace that we were here. Quietly," he told her. He gathered the stack of electronic mail printouts and separated the last page from the rest of the ream by tearing carefully along the perforated line.

Lee hadn't moved. "Lee?" Brad whispered. She looked spooked. He hadn't been really worried until he saw the look on her face. "Lianna."

"I can't be caught in here," she said. "I'm not even a student. I'm trespassing, and my dad . . ."

"At least you're a minor. I'm eighteen. I can be arrested and charged as an adult for breaking and entering, not to mention computer hacking." He took a deep breath. "We'll be fine, but we have to put the office back into order."

He gently steered Lee back into the front office and helped her gather the photocopies she'd made and return the folders to their file cabinets. Satisfied that it wouldn't be immediately apparent that anyone had been here, he eased the door to the hall open—and froze. He heard footsteps coming toward them.

He closed the door again, holding the doorknob and slowly turning it to latch it without making noise. Lee raised her eyebrows.

"Too late. Guard's coming," he mouthed.

Her eyes went wide. She rushed to the window and yanked it open.

"Lee!" he whispered. "No!" He followed her.

She leaned out onto the sill, and he grabbed her waist. She shrieked.

"Are you nuts?" he asked.

"Let go!" She kicked back at him, but he didn't let go until he pulled her back.

"We can't jump," he said.

"I'm not going to jump, dummy. I'm getting rid of this stuff." She picked up a thick folder of papers she had copied.

"Oh, yeah," Brad said. "You're really good at this. I can't believe it's your first time."

"I never said I haven't done this before," Lee said.

He whispered to Nick, "We're dropping some stuff out the window. Can you collect it? We might get caught, but it would help if we aren't discovered with the evidence."

"Roger," Nick said. "Bombs away."

Lee wrapped a rubber band from the assistant's desk around the folder. Brad followed her lead, rolling his thick stack of print-outs into a tube and securing it with another rubber band. Then they held the packages out the window and dropped them. A moment later they heard a thud and rustle as they landed in the foliage below. Brad glanced down and saw Nick heading for the hedge.

Brad spotted the duffel bag peeking out from under the assistant's desk. "Oh, shit." He grabbed it and tossed it out the window too. He heard a thump and an "Ow!"

The walkie-talkie blared: "What the hell?! Over!"

"Sorry." Brad leaned out the window. Below, Nick was

chasing after a few pages that had gotten free of Lee's folder. "I guess it isn't that far down . . . ," he said.

They were only on the second floor, but they were *tall* stories. He shook his head and closed the window. "Should we try to hide?"

They heard keys jingle outside the door. Lee blinked, and just like that, her fear seemed to have washed away, and she was as confident as ever. "Just play along," she said.

A key slid into the lock. The doorknob turned.

Lee grabbed Brad, pulled him toward her, and kissed him. It only took him a second to lean into it and pretend to be making out with her.

They were totally pretending.

They didn't separate until the lights came on and the guard cleared his throat. The man was short, with a broad, almost cartoonish mustache. His arms were crossed over a big belly.

"What are you kids doing in here?" he asked gruffly, with a light Italian accent.

"What does it look like?" Lee asked.

His expression hardened. "Look, you're not supposed to be here."

"Sure I am," Lee said. "Or else how did I get in? My daddy works here."

"Your . . . dad?" The guard looked apprehensive.

"Hello? President of the school? He said I could use his computer to finish work on a project for class."

"So who's this?" The guard jerked his head toward Brad.

Lee grinned. "My study partner." She squeezed Brad's hand.

Brad hesitated, trying to remember the name of the president's daughter . . . He'd overheard Sovern talking about her to his wife on the phone earlier that day. Elizabeth!

"Liz, you said it would be okay." Brad slurred his words slightly, as if he were drunk or stoned. She hid a smile.

"It's fine, Brad." Lee rolled her eyes.

"I'm going to have to call this in," the guard said.

"Go ahead," Lee said. "Call my father and tell him you interrupted his daughter Elizabeth's school assignment the night before it's due. Do you have his number? It's 212-854-7942. That'll ring right by his bed and wake him up. He's a light sleeper, and it takes him three hours to fall back to sleep, by the way."

The guard looked concerned.

"Then he 'accidentally' wakes up Mother too, because you know, and she doesn't get any sleep either."

Brad shook his head slightly. *Too much, Lee*, he thought.

"But if you do me a favor, I won't raise much of a stink with Daddy."

The guard's eyes narrowed. "What kind of favor?"

"Not much. Only . . . you don't need to mention Brad, do you?" Lee batted her eyes innocently.

"Hey, we're pretty much done here. Maybe we should just go," Brad said in a low, conciliatory voice.

Lee's face lit up as if he'd just suggested they all go for ice-cream sundaes. "That's a great idea. Hey, what's your name, sir?" she asked the guard.

Flustered, he responded, "J-jack. Jack Hughes." Then he clamped his mouth shut and looked worried.

"Mr. Hughes. What do you say my friend and I just leave and neither of us have to mention this to my father?"

"Please, sir?" Brad said. He stretched the last word out, "Surrrre . . . ," and then giggled. He reached for Lee, and she slapped him away.

Hughes licked his lips and looked from Lee to Brad. He looked around the office, trying to figure out if anything was missing or broken or whatever. Maybe looking for an indication of what they'd really been doing. He pursed his lips, probably not wanting to think about it too much.

Hughes's shoulders relaxed. "All right, but I have to escort you out."

"Thank you *so* much!" Lee said cheerfully.

"Thank you, thank you, thank you," Brad said. He really was grateful that the deception had worked.

Only it was too soon to be relieved; they weren't out of there yet. And as the elevator doors opened, the walkie-talkie tucked under his shirt emitted a burst of static, and Nick whispered, "You guys okay?"

Lee froze. Brad pushed her out of the elevator. "Run!" he said. He slapped the Door Close button on his way out, catching a stunned look on Hughes's face. He ran pell-mell after Lee toward the exit, only hearing a strangled "Hey!" from Hughes belatedly.

"Split up," Brad shouted.

Lee burst out the front doors, Brad right behind her. He leaped down the handful of stairs and hit the cobblestones running. He stumbled on the uneven ground, but he didn't stop. Lee took a right toward East Campus, and he spun left heading for his dorm. He cast a quick glance back and saw Hughes watching him from the doorway. He'd apparently given up the chase, unless he'd already called for backup.

Brad pressed Talk on his walkie. "Nick, get out of here!"

"Way ahead of you, B," Nick said. "See you back at the ranch. Over."

Brad grimaced. Of course Nick had watched out for himself. It was the right call, taking off with the evidence, but it still bugged him that he'd left his friends behind. Rather, his randomly selected college roommate and girlfriend.

Strike that. A girl who was basically a stranger—to both of them. And there was a low chance of her ever being his girlfriend. . . . He bet after all this, he would never hear from Lee Monroe again.

Brad had been wrong before. Lee called him as soon as she'd finished reviewing the files she'd collected from Nick after their great escape. She wanted to meet.

Brad sipped a frosty Broadway shake in a booth at Tom's Diner as he waited for her to show up. Until she walked in the door, he hadn't been certain she would really appear. She scanned the seats, and he raised his hand to catch her attention. He kept it raised until she made it to his table.

"Yes, Mr. Stein. Do you have to go to the bathroom?" she said.

"Huh?" he asked.

"Your hand. Which of us is still in high school?" She put a hand on her hip and grinned.

"Oh." He dropped his hand to the table with a short laugh.

She looked completely different from how he'd seen her before. Her hair was pulled back into a ponytail that made her look fourteen. Which wasn't much younger than her real age, he reminded himself. When she shrugged out of her red peacoat, he saw she was wearing a white blouse and a gray skirt.

She hung her coat beside his on the booth's coat hook. "Nick's not here yet?" Did she seem relieved that Brad was alone?

"He isn't coming. He's decided it's a lot safer to work from behind his keyboard. And he's excited about something he's working on."

Nick had been deep diving into the Columbia servers, using the administrative access Brad had gotten him. When he got like that, he barely went to classes or remembered to eat, and Brad didn't think too long about the two plastic two-liter bottles of Mountain Dew under his desk; the level of liquid in one bottle seemed to go down while the other went up over the course of a few days.

Brad somehow had the strange feeling that Nick had

manipulated him into helping him instead of the other way around. He also felt slightly guilty about exposing Columbia to a curious and skilled hacker, but Nick was a good guy. He wouldn't do anything *too* illegal . . . probably.

Lee slid into the booth and grabbed the silver tumbler with the rest of Brad's shake. She tipped it backward and sipped. Brad's eyebrows shot up.

"What is this?" She licked her lips.

"You mean what *was* that? Broadway shake. Coffee and vanilla." He slid one of the sticky menus over to her. "I also ordered us some disco fries."

She pushed the menu aside. "Perfect." She reached into her backpack and retrieved a familiar folder stuffed with evidence on Columbia's financial investments in South Africa.

"Have you decided what to do with all that?" he asked.

"Have you read the electronic mail messages you forwarded?"

"I haven't had a chance to," Brad lied.

She nodded thoughtfully. "I'm not sure how to handle this information."

"Nick and I have been talking about it. I'm thinking you should send it to the *Columbia Spectator*, and tell them that you'll also be forwarding copies to the *New York Times* and other local papers a few days later."

She opened the folder and turned easily to a page that showed an electronic mail header. She stared down at it. "That's definitely an option," she said. "Could we do it anonymously?"

"I'm not sure that would work. Like it or not, we're part of the story, aren't we? Without us to lend credibility, who will trust it?"

The waiter brought over a plate of disco fries, and Lee slapped the folder shut.

The cheese was already congealing on the top, but that didn't deter her. She snatched a fry and crammed it into her mouth. When the waiter asked if she wanted anything, she ordered another Broadway shake and a slice of pecan pie.

Lee lowered her voice. "It would be even more of a problem if we wanted to bring the info to a TV station. Any other ideas?"

"Nick had one suggestion. . . ." Brad shook his head.

"What?"

He looked around. Started whispering. "We already have access to President Sovern's account. We could do what we already did, send all those messages out with an explanation, but blast it to everyone with an electronic mail account. Then everyone would know."

"But that's only going to reach everyone on campus."

"The students and faculty would hold the university accountable."

"I haven't seen them out there, marching with us," Lee said. "If we sent that message, they'll know right away that the system has been hacked, and they may even be able to trace it to you."

Brad nodded. He tasted a soggy french fry, then pushed the platter over to Lee. "Nick isn't keen on that approach, but he did offer to help. He'd hate to lose the foot he has in their door, but otherwise his plan seems like the best option." That was another reason Nick had been working nonstop to worm his way into the heart of the system.

They sat in silence for a while as they brainstormed.

"I suppose . . ." Brad looked right at Lee. "We also could do *nothing* with the info."

She closed her eyes. "That crossed my mind too."

"Maybe we could let the board know, anonymously, that we have this information, and we can threaten to release it if they don't step up their divestment plan."

Her eyes fluttered open. "That sounds promising. Tell me more."

"I'm just riffing here, but like, we sort of blackmail them. Share enough that they know we're telling the truth, and then put it on them to either come clean themselves or make good and do the right thing."

Lee's head was bobbing up and down. "I like it. That could work."

Brad took a deep breath. "This way, your father doesn't need to know you're involved," he said gently.

She sat straighter. "You did see his messages."

"Yeah."

"Why didn't you say anything? Why didn't you try to stop me?"

"Because it's your decision, Lee. And I think you've made a good one. Even if this doesn't work out, maybe it's enough that you tried. When so many others ignored the issues, or decided it wasn't their fight, you came through. For strangers, people you'll likely never meet." Brad grinned. "That's . . . *awesome.* You're awesome."

Lee's face flushed with pink. "Thanks, but it doesn't feel like I'm doing enough."

Lee poured her own Broadway shake into her glass, and Brad sneaked her metal tumbler away. He dipped his straw in and drank the rest of her shake loudly. She stuck out her tongue at him.

"You're doing more than your classmates," he said.

"Right? They are the most apolitical group of spoiled brats I've ever met. All they care about is celebrity gossip and doing their hair and reading fashion magazines, which is stupid because we have to wear these uniforms every day." Lee's nostrils flared when she was worked up, Brad noticed. He smiled.

"What?" she asked.

"You're just ahead of your time, is all," he said. "Speaking of which, I was thinking that maybe Nick is onto something after all, with this computer activism idea."

Brad outlined what he'd been thinking, about how they could use electronic mail to coordinate with and mobilize students at universities, maybe even collaborate with them to put forth a bigger effort. Lee was excited.

"We can use it to advocate, share information, reach a lot farther than just the city without waiting for the national papers and news to pick up the story." Lee stared at her untouched plate of pie. Her expression sobered. "We could have used something like that when news about that massacre in South Africa broke last week. Everyone should have been marching then."

Brad hadn't even heard about any massacre, but he was still new at this. He'd only just picked up a newspaper this morning, in his first attempt to pay more attention to what was going on, in the world around him . . . and right in front of him.

"The best thing is, you can even help organize rallies and protests safely," he said. "Anonymously, even."

"We could do so much! There are lots of other important causes out there, and if we aren't limited by geography, we can support them from anywhere in the world. Only . . . I don't actually have an electronic mail account of my own yet. I keep bugging Dad for it, but I know he'd want to be able to track what I'm doing online."

"'Big Brother is Watching You,'" Brad said.

"Nothing is your own except the few cubic centimeters inside your skull," she paraphrased.

They smiled stupidly at each other for a while.

"But seriously, can we do this?" she asked.

Brad nodded. "I can get you set up with your own mail account. Even a columbia.edu address, until you really enroll." He winked at her.

"Sure, that stuff too," she said.

That stuff? She wasn't talking about her activist efforts now? *Oh.*

"Oh," he said.

"I forgot to mention, you really impressed me back there." She dipped a finger into the ketchup and drew a little squiggle on her plate.

"Maybe I have a promising future in breaking and entering," Brad said.

"I was referring to us kissing," she said.

"Oh," Brad said. His face flushed.

"There could be a promising future in that, too . . . unless the high school thing is a problem?"

He shook his head.

"Okay, then." She picked up the bill. "I'm going to go pay this. No, don't worry, it's the least I can do. And then, you can walk me home."

"You come up with the best plans," he said.

He waited for Lee outside with their coats and helped her into hers. "Where's home?" he asked.

"Seventy-Fifth and Central Park West," she said.

"That's quite a walk," he said. "Could take a while."

"Good," she said. "I do my best thinking on my feet. Oh, and there's a great movie theater on the way. Do you read Lovecraft, or just Orwell?"

Brad knew that Lovecraft had been a horror author, but he hadn't ever read anything by him. Unlike Orwell's *1984*, it wasn't required reading in high school.

"No, I love . . . Lovecraft."

"Then we have to watch *Re-Animator*! I've already seen it twice. It's sick."

Brad smiled uncertainly. "Great." He hated horror movies, but maybe they wouldn't have to watch the whole thing, especially if she'd already seen it. . . .

"Hey, is this a date?" he asked.

"Is it?" Lee asked.

"Isn't it?" he said.

"We've already kissed and had dinner together and you're walking me home, so we seem to be doing this backward."

"We also broke into an administrator's office, stole some files, and are planning to blackmail a university board of trustees. I think we're making this up as we go along," Brad said. "I'll just keep following your lead."

Lianna grinned. "Do try to keep up."

Praise for

THE SILENCE OF SIX:

"Suspenseful. . . . Along with pleasing fans of Cory Doctorow's
Homeland and like 'hacktion' thrillers, this offers sobering
insight into how fragile our privacy really is."
—ALA *Booklist*

"The suspense is palpable in this tour de force mixture of
mystery and computer technology that takes readers inside the
weird world of hackers and top level secrets. A classic puzzler
with a twenty-first century twist."
—Michael Cart (*Booklist* columnist)

"An entertaining and exciting book with non-stop action. . . .
[A] hard-to-put-down read."
—The Examiner.com

"I highly recommend *The Silence of Six* to anyone looking for a book and a thrill ride in one perfectly executed package."
—Teen Reads

"This gripping thriller takes readers into the hidden world of hacktivism. They will be forced to consider what their privacy means to them. What kinds of causes are we willing to die for, and how far should we go to fight back against those who want to spy on every aspect of our lives? The choices Max and his allies have to make are difficult ones, and readers will appreciate the courage he has to summon up to follow in the footsteps of his friend."
—Looking Glass Review

"Amazing, amazing book. I recommend this to everyone, not only to those who are tech-geeks but to everyone."
—The Booklandia

"With a story built around advanced technology and government conspiracy that is close enough to reach out and touch, *The Silence of Six* will keep you up all night turning pages!"
—Julie Cross, international bestselling author of the Tempest series

Praise for

AGAINST ALL SILENCE:

"*Against All Silence* had the action, excitement, and travel of an adult cyber thriller, but with teenagers fully embroiled in the action. The content and situations will catch young readers' attention and keep them reading and rooting for Max and his crew. Highly recommended."
—Goodreads review

"The language isn't complex and technical specifics are somewhat glossed over, with Myers only giving the bare minimum of jargon needed to keep the plot moving forward. This makes it approachable as a thriller with geek overtones, with much of the action having the feeling of a spy novel. The

pacing is even and Myers does a good job of weaving in of the moment themes like Internet freedom, privacy and social activism."
—Takes on Tech

"Bits of it even remind me of George Orwell's *1984*. I would recommend you check this book out for yourself!"
—Jagged Edge Reviews

"Non-techie readers will enjoy the story immensely and come away with just a bit more knowledge of how the whole internet world works."
—PamelaKramer.com

"Just like the first book in the series, it is jam-packed with action. This time, however, the stakes are even higher. "
—Devin's Book Hub

"Myers' writing captures the reader's curiosity and interest with the mystery and thrill as the plot develops. The character development is also really good."
—The Booklandia

"*Against All Silence* is a fun read that combines thriller with computer hacking knowledge. Think of it like a little *Mr. Robot* of the YA world."
—BSC Kids